# His Wyoming Baby Blessing

## Jill Kemerer

D0106809

⟨H⟩ HARLEQUIN® LOVE INSPIRED®

Recycling programs
for this product may
not exist in your area.

LOVE INSPIRED BOOKS

ISBN-13: 978-1-335-42885-1

His Wyoming Baby Blessing

www.Harlequin.com

Printed in U.S.A.

## "I don't want to be a bother..."

"You won't be a bother. That's why I'm going to hang out with you. I miss you." Wade didn't realize how much he meant it until he said it.

"I'll be boring to be around, anyhow. I've taken napping to a whole new level." Kit flashed him a half-hearted smile and averted her eyes.

She was lying. He knew her too well.

"You're sleeping pretty good, then?"

He'd been right to take the time off. Kit wasn't sleeping. Her mind was probably racing circles around the baby's health troubles. Or she was mourning Cam. Both, most likely.

Wade might not be able to fix any of it, but he could be present.

Kit needed a friend.

And, frankly, so did he.

It was only for a week. Nothing to worry about.

Then they'd go back to being long-distance friends. The way it should be.

Why didn't the thought fill him with relief?

He wasn't in a position to take care of Kit. He couldn't even take care of himself. He had to tread carefully...

**Jill Kemerer** writes novels with love, humor and faith. Besides spoiling her mini dachshund and keeping up with her busy kids, Jill reads stacks of books, lives for her morning coffee and gushes over fluffy animals. She resides in Ohio with her husband and two children. Jill loves connecting with readers, so please visit her website, jillkemerer.com, or contact her at PO Box 2802, Whitehouse, OH 43571.

## Books by Jill Kemerer

### Love Inspired

#### *Wyoming Cowboys*

*The Rancher's Mistletoe Bride*
*Reunited with the Bull Rider*
*Wyoming Christmas Quadruplets*
*His Wyoming Baby Blessing*

*Small-Town Bachelor*
*Unexpected Family*
*Her Small-Town Romance*
*Yuletide Redemption*
*Hometown Hero's Redemption*

Visit the Author Profile page at Harlequin.com.

Now the God of hope fill you with all joy and peace in believing, that ye may abound in hope, through the power of the Holy Ghost.

—*Romans* 15:13

To the AW baseball moms!
Sandi Hood and Kerri Penrod—
you've taken the brunt of my plotting nonsense
and iced-coffee addiction—thank you!
Special thanks to Amy, Jill, Rhonda, Kim W.,
Kim K., Marla, Dawn, Michelle, Dreama, Katie,
Heather, Amber, Brooke and Jessica for your
encouragement, pictures and smiles. My sincere
apologies to anyone I might have missed!

Thank you to Shana, Melissa and Elizabeth,
the editors who helped shape this book.
You make me a better writer.

And finally, thank you to my agent, Rachel Kent,
for all you do.

# Chapter One

She should have been here by now.

Wade Croft paced the front porch of the sprawling log cabin he called home. Late May wildflowers and blue skies spread as far as he could see, pausing only at the white-capped Bighorn Mountains. Unfortunately, the peaceful scene did nothing to slow his rapid heartbeat. Kit McAllistor would be here any minute, and the last time he'd seen her had been at her husband's funeral four months ago. The experience had unsettled him.

Kit's stricken, drawn face as she'd cried over the casket had picked off the scab on emotions he'd gotten used to pretending didn't exist, and, as much as he sympathized with her loss, he'd avoided contacting her since then. The little girl he'd met in foster care all those years ago—his childhood best friend, the one who always believed the best in him—had grown into a very special, very beautiful woman.

Her husband passing away complicated things.

A dust cloud formed in the distance. It must be Kit's car. He propped his hand against one of the posts. His land stretched for miles. Land he'd been blessed with. He'd taken it for granted in his quest to expand. Look where it had gotten him. On the brink of losing it all. Why had he overextended himself last year to buy Dudley Farms, a massive farm east of here? If he didn't find a buyer for Dudley Farms soon, he'd lose everything, including his home, JPX Ranch.

Somehow, he'd find a way to get out of this financial hole, and until he did, no one needed to know about the trouble he was in.

Right now he had to focus on Kit.

The compact silver car stopped in front of the garage. He had the oddest sensation that if he moved even a muscle, his life would change forever.

*Nonsense. Get over there like the barn is on fire!*

He took off toward the driveway as the car door shut with a thud. Kit walked his way. A perfectly rounded belly jutted out from her long sundress.

His feet refused to move another inch.

She was pregnant.

Why the concept floored him, he couldn't say, maybe because the thought of her having a baby hadn't occurred to him, with Cam's death and all.

If he thought her husband dying complicated things...

"Wade." The word sounded scratchy, defeated. Her skin was drawn, dark crescents shadowed her pale green eyes and weariness burdened her shoulders. The woman standing before him barely resembled his vibrant friend.

"Kitty Cat." The old nickname fell off his tongue before he could worry about the consequences.

Something sparked in her eyes, and she closed the distance between them, wrapping her arms around his waist. He held her lightly, trying to ignore the sensations crowding his brain. Soft skin. Long silky hair with a hint of coconut shampoo. A pregnant tummy separating them. She seemed thinner, not taking into account the baby. There was a frailness to her that didn't mesh with any version of the Kit he knew. At least the freckles on her nose were still there.

"I didn't know where else to go." She stepped back and let out the most pitiful sigh he'd ever heard.

"What have I always told you?" He tried to capture the teasing tone he saved especially for her, but he didn't quite nail it.

"If I ever need anything, you're here for me." She didn't crack a smile. In fact, her face was as devoid of expression as it was of makeup.

"Exactly." He straightened, locking his jaw. The fragile, pregnant woman standing here wasn't the feisty, optimistic girl he'd bonded with as a kid. Life had beaten her down. It had beaten him down enough, too, but he hated that it hadn't spared her.

"Come inside." He held the door open, then he led the way to the great room, a large open space with plenty of windows, hardwood floors, leather furniture and area rugs to keep the chill out. Visible signs of the wealth he'd accumulated and, in his greed, put in jeopardy.

"You really did it, didn't you?" She looked around, lowering her body onto one of the couches. "You always said you were going to own the biggest ranch in Wyoming someday. Your house alone is massive."

A surge of shame filled him. If he hadn't bought Dudley Farms, he'd have been financially set for a lifetime. All attempts at trying to salvage his mistake hadn't worked.

Last year the farm's old irrigation equipment had failed, and the drought had polished off any hopes of growing enough crops to be profitable. On both properties—here on JPX Ranch and on Dudley Farms—he'd downsized all his employees to the bare minimum. Sold as many calves, heifers and horses as he could, except for his favorite stud horse, Del Poncho. He'd sell Del Poncho only if absolutely necessary. But the way the bills were coming in, he'd have to sooner rather than later.

"I didn't realize you were...having a baby." He waved in her general direction as he sat in a chair opposite her. "I mean, it was hard enough Cam died." Heat licked up his neck, and he averted his gaze. What was wrong with him? He wasn't shy. Didn't get squeamish. And here he was acting like a pimply kid instead of a grown man.

She tucked her hair behind her ear and averted her own eyes. It brought him back to their younger days. She'd been eight and he'd been ten when they'd met at a foster home.

They'd been best buds the three years they'd lived there. He could still see the freckles on her nose as she swung her legs high in the air, brown hair flying in the wind. Her eyes had danced with delight as she begged him to push her higher, higher. When her swing would finally come to a stop, he'd sit on the one next to hers, and, with their legs dangling, they'd talk about the future.

He'd been set on owning the biggest ranch in Wyoming. He'd have so much money no one could ever again tell him what to do. She was going to be a teacher and get married to the best husband in the world and have two boys, one girl, a dog, a cat and a nice house. They both had been on their way to achieving those dreams. And though they still shared a childhood bond, Kit's marriage to Cam had strained their friendship. Wade understood. Marriage changed things.

"I guess the perfect family you always wanted isn't turning out the way you'd hoped," he said, as gently as possible.

"Yeah, well, it was a stupid dream, anyhow." She gazed out the wall of windows. Sadness and something else was etched into her face. Bitterness?

Not Kit. Sunny, kind, spitfire Kit never let anything get her down.

He didn't like to think of her spirit broken, but maybe he was overanalyzing things.

"When are you due?"

"October second." Her shrug gave him the impression she was nervous. "Depending."

Depending on what? He scuffed his foot against the floor.

"Thanks for letting me stay here. It will only be for a week. The extended-stay hotel should have a room for me by then."

She hadn't given him much information when she called last night. Just said she needed a place to stay for a week and did he have a spare room for her? He'd offered her one of several renovated cabins on his property. They'd been remodeled a few years ago for his friends to use for getaways, hunting, fishing…whatever. She was welcome to hunker down in any of them.

But last night she hadn't mentioned an extended-stay hotel.

She also hadn't mentioned she was having a baby.

"Why are you going to some roadhouse?" He needed more information from her. Nothing was adding up, and he didn't exactly consider himself slow.

One of her shoulders lifted. "I'm moving to Casper."

"Did you get a new job or something?" He couldn't picture her accepting a different position. She loved teaching second grade in Fort Laramie. But maybe the memories with Cam made it too hard for her to continue working there.

"No." Her hands covered her tummy.

Her short answers, air of gloom and lack of animation kicked up his stomach acid.

"Kit, this is me. You don't have to hide anything." He leaned forward, immediately recognizing the hypocrisy of his words. He was hiding his problems from her and everyone else he was close to. "What is going on?"

"I need a new start."

Normally, he'd buy what she was saying. She'd lost the love of her life. She was alone. Pregnant. But…she was keeping secrets. He narrowed his eyes. "You're not telling me everything."

"Look, I need a place to crash for a few days, and then I'll be on my way. Don't ask me to tell you my life story in the meantime."

"I already know your life story." He knew most of it. The important stuff, anyhow.

"That was the old me."

"I liked the old you."

"Well, she's gone, so don't bother looking for her. Why don't you show me the cabin where I can put my stuff? Then you can go back to work." She braced both hands against the couch cushions in an attempt to get up. He sprang to his feet, offering her his hand.

"Why the hotel? Why Casper?" He kept her hand in his and searched her face for clues about whatever she wrestled with. Had Cam's death destroyed the best part of her?

Her eyes welled with tears.

Great, he'd made her cry. Why had he badgered her? Of course she wanted to move. She was alone and pregnant and grieving the sudden death of her husband. No wonder she was shattered and prickly. He'd always tried to fix anything bothering her, but this was beyond him.

Maybe he should do as she asked. Take her to the cabin and leave her alone to work things out.

"It's the baby," she whispered.

"What do you mean?" He gently clasped her forearms and bent to look into her eyes.

"He has a large hole in his heart."

"What?"

"A few weeks ago, I had a routine ultrasound. I figured I'd be finding out if it was a boy or girl, and everything would be fine. Unfortunately, they suspected there was a hole in his heart, but they told me not to worry and to come back in a few weeks for a fetal echocardiogram. Well, I did, and the hole was confirmed, which led to another ultrasound with a specialist last Wednesday. Since the heart defect may be caused by chromosome abnormalities, I had an amniocentesis done on Friday. They're using the cells to do a chromosomal microarray test to check for Down syndrome, DiGeorge syndrome and a few other things. The results won't be in for about three weeks."

He let go of her arms. Friday. And today was Tuesday. Chromosomes, tests, a hole in the baby's heart…*his* heart, she'd said.

The baby was a boy.

An image came to mind of a little tyke with Kit's freckles holding Wade's hand as the child stared up at him with excitement at the thought of riding around the ranch.

"This amnio-cent-whats-is and chromosome thing—what does all of it mean?"

"Amniocentesis is a test to determine the likelihood of genetic problems. It was offered in my first trimester, but I opted not to have it at that time because I'm young and healthy. And chromosome abnormalities are just a fancy way of saying my baby might have special needs." Her inhalation was long and shaky.

"Okay, we'll deal with it." The earlier image of a little boy morphed from one who looked like Kit to one with Down syndrome. The image appealed to him as much as the first one had.

"The hole could heal on its own." A tear dropped onto her cheek, and she swiped it away. "But if not, the baby will require heart surgery. And if he has DiGeorge syndrome, there's a strong chance he won't make it to his first birthday. The doctor told me not to worry about DiGeorge too much and that heart defects are common, but I don't know what to think at this point. I'll know more after the test results come back. In the meantime, I'm praying he doesn't die in the womb."

*Die?* He tried to process it. No wonder she'd become a shadow of her former self.

She'd lost her husband, and now she might lose her baby, too.

"I'm scared, Wade." The faint words spun him out of his thoughts.

He understood scared. Too many sleepless nights trying to come up with a solution to his lack of cash flow had taken their toll.

"You're staying here until the baby is born. Not in a hotel." He straightened, widening his stance. "I want you to rest. You won't move a muscle. I'll take care of you."

Why had he promised the last part? Him? Taking care of her? He could barely keep up with the mortgage on his land. He didn't trust himself to take care of a stray dog at this point.

"No." She clutched her hands, wringing them together.

"If he does have special needs, would you still want him?" he asked.

"Of course! I just want him to live. I don't care what problems he might have. I love this baby so much. I can't bear to think of him dying."

He wasn't surprised. She'd love any child fiercely, but her declaration reminded him of those complications from earlier.

Kit wasn't his. Never had been, never would be.

And that's the way it would stay. She deserved someone who would treat her right and take care of her financially and emotionally. He'd never been good at the emotional stuff, and, frankly, he had little to give in the finance department, either.

He'd just have to do his best to support her, regardless.

"Stay here in the main house. I have three guest rooms. That way if you need me—"

"No. I need space." She shook her head rapidly, her long brown hair swishing behind her. "I appreciate the offer, but I can't. One of your cabins will be fine."

"You can take your pick. Stay in one of them until the baby is born."

"That's kind of you, but I'll just stay the week." She ducked her chin. "I'm only crashing here until the hotel has a vacancy."

He should be relieved. It wasn't as if he could offer her anything more than a temporary place to stay. As much as he'd like to see her taken care of long-term, it wasn't his place.

"If you'll point me in the right direction..."

He gave her a curt nod. "I'll take you over there right now."

JPX Ranch truly was her last resort. On the long drive here, Kit had dreaded having to rely on Wade. She'd messed up her life, and he'd always been able to see right through her. But as she followed his truck down a dirt driveway behind his house, relief replaced the dread. He was the one person—the only one—she'd ever been able to count on for anything.

And here he was, coming through for her again.

If he had any idea what a disaster her life had been for the past three years, would he view her the same?

She had no intention of finding out.

Wade stopped in front of a large log cabin. She could see four other smaller structures spaced out farther down the lane. As she got out of her car, she was glad the blooming wildflowers had spread to surround the guest homes. Silver lupine and little yellow castles waved in the breeze, and she couldn't help but enjoy their beauty. For a moment, anyway. Nothing good in her life ever stuck around for long.

"I think you'll like this one the best." Strength oozed from him as he strode up the covered porch, then swung open the door and waited for her to join him.

She tried not to stare. In form-fitting jeans, cowboy boots and a short-sleeved Western shirt, he looked every bit the cowboy most women only dreamed about. His blue eyes crinkled at the corners—a side effect of his sense of humor. He kept his dark blond hair short. The bone structure of his face was perfectly symmetrical, and she'd often thought he could model for one of those rodeo calendars she'd hung on her wall as a teen. Not that she'd ever tell him that. Most days his head was too big for his cowboy hat without her swelling it even more.

What woman wasn't attracted to Wade Croft? Even one on her deathbed would likely revive if it meant catching a glimpse of the prime Wyoming cowboy.

The cabin was anything but the dusty old hunting lodge she'd expected. Freshly renovated with big windows, gleaming wood floors and comfortable furniture, it was nicer than any place she'd lived. And, better yet, it held none of the bad memories or mistakes she'd made in her other homes.

"It's so light and open." The high wooden ceilings cast a pretty glow on the room.

"The kitchen's back here. Should meet your needs."

She followed him and stopped, her mouth dropping open.

"You're kidding, right?" She trailed her fingertips along the marble—or was it quartz? It certainly wasn't the chipped counters she was used to. This was hands down the best kitchen she'd ever seen. With stainless steel appliances, tall cabinets and a pretty backsplash, it was her ideal kitchen.

From the window above the sink, a carpet of wildflowers came into view. A reprieve for her weary soul.

"Kidding? What do you mean?" His defensive tone would have made her laugh if she still had a shred of joy left, which she didn't. Not by a long shot. "What's wrong with the cabin?"

"Not a single thing." She could at least attempt to set him at ease. He'd been kind today. But then, he'd always been kind to her. "Except your boots are leaving dirt all over the floor."

He kicked up the bottom of his boot, then shot her a teasing glare. "My boots are as clean as the day I took them out of the box."

"You sure about that?"

"As sure as I am a hotel won't do you a lick of good."

*The hotel. Right.*

She massaged her belly. Until recently,

she'd been dealing with Cam's death as best as she could, but finding out about the hole in the baby's heart and learning it might be caused by special needs… As much as she hoped the hole would heal on its own, the fact the doctor was running all those tests didn't reassure her. Nor did the online research she'd done on her own.

"Does this place have a bedroom?" She forced a tight smile. The sooner Wade concluded the tour, the sooner she could sit and think. Well, worry and fret about the baby was more like it.

His forehead furrowed as if he wanted to press the issue. "Down the hall. I'll show you."

The bedroom had log walls, traditional furniture, a neutral area rug and a puffy white comforter on top of a king-size bed.

"The television works. Bathroom is attached." He paused in the doorway with one hand planted on the frame. His long body filled the space. "Tell me what you need."

What did she need?

*A healthy baby.* Well, that wasn't entirely true. Even if the child *wasn't* healthy, she still wanted him. She could handle the hole in the heart, the special needs. What she really needed was a *living* baby. She just wanted a chance to raise him. No matter what complications were involved.

Her life had been one big complication for years. For her entire life, really. With each change, she'd dug her feet in, disciplined herself to be good, to meet other people's needs in the hopes they'd keep her around.

And every single time, she hadn't been good enough.

The sincerity radiating from Wade's expression tempted her to confess the truth about why Cam had died, but she hadn't survived an abusive aunt, four foster homes and a cheating husband for nothing.

"I'm pretty tired." She sat on the edge of the bed. If Wade wasn't here, she'd crawl under the covers and sleep for a month. Try to, at least.

"Stretch out and rest. I'll get your bags." He knocked on the door frame and left.

She was too tired to protest. Besides, Wade was a strapping cowboy. He'd never let her haul her suitcases and bags inside. She had nothing to prove by overexerting herself and everything to lose if she let her pride override her common sense.

This baby needed a healthy mama.

Her idea of a perfect family had been shattered long ago. She'd give about anything to have any family—perfect or not. A family of two suited her fine. Her and her boy.

*Please, God, let my baby live.*

The front door creaked, and Wade's footsteps clomped closer. He set two suitcases in the bedroom. The muscles in his arms and chest strained as he straightened. Even pregnant, she couldn't help but notice. Unfortunately, her pulse did, too.

"Be right back with the rest." He waved his fingers toward the bed. "Why aren't you lying down?"

"I don't need to lie down. Now scoot." She

was surprised how easily she fell into their familiar sassing, but it left a bittersweet tang on her tongue.

His lips curved into a cocky smile as he exited the room.

She wished she could be the same Kit McAllistor she was before Cam had announced he wanted a divorce. The one who could banter with her old friend Wade, the one who believed love conquered all and if she just tried hard enough, her husband would want her and not other women.

The old Kit wouldn't have screamed at Cam the night he had a heart attack and died.

She might not have killed him, but it was her fault he was dead. If she hadn't yelled those terrible things, he wouldn't have had the heart attack. He still would have divorced her, though.

The old Kit was gone, along with her dreams and her husband.

No matter what happened, she was on her own. Deluding herself into thinking Cam would provide the security she'd craved had been her biggest mistake. She couldn't afford to make the same one twice.

"That's everything." Wade deposited the bags and wiped his hands down his jeans. "You hungry?"

She almost said no, but her stomach growled.

"Guess that answers my question." He hitched his chin for her to follow him. "Come on. I'll take you back to my place and feed you."

Why tears sprang to her eyes, she didn't know. Maybe because with all the uncertainties she faced—no job, no husband, a baby with serious health problems—she could still count on Wade.

"What are we having?" She stood, pressing her palm into her lower back. The drive had tightened every muscle in her poor body.

"Steak." He rolled his eyes. "Du-uh."

"Grilled?" Her mouth started watering. The man had always been able to grill a mean steak. "With melted butter on top?"

"As if I'd cook it any other way."

A steak. Warm bed. Gourmet kitchen. And wildflowers as far as the eye could see.

She didn't deserve this.

One week.

Then back to the real world.

She'd build a new life. In Casper. With her sweet baby. If he lived…

For now, she'd do her best to get through the next seven days. "Lead the way."

## Chapter Two

If he could find a way back to the easy
friendship he'd enjoyed with Kit over the
years, their first supper together wouldn't be
awkward. Well, not as awkward as it was at
the moment. It was hard to believe she was
actually sitting across from him at his dining table.

The top of her rounded stomach was barely
visible from where he sat. Why her being
pregnant messed with his head so much, he
couldn't say, but it brought out weird feelings. Protectiveness and worry and…never
mind about the rest.

He'd practically grown up with her, they'd

been friends for so long. They relied on each other, but not in a romantic way. She'd always viewed him as a big brother, and he'd considered her a...

He took another bite of steak and chewed a little too aggressively.

So he'd had a crush on her and lived for her emails and calls all through high school, even though they'd been apart.

And big deal, he'd visited her every chance he could get when she was at college.

The day she'd called and told him she'd gotten engaged had been like a big cow patty to the face for him. But he'd congratulated her, hung up, dusted off his chaps, gotten back in the saddle and ridden out to the section of fence he'd been about to replace. He may have chopped an old post into tiny bits that afternoon, but by the next morning, he'd been fine.

"Is Casper temporary? Are you moving back to Fort Laramie after the baby is born?" He sprinkled pepper on his baked potato.

"No." Her eyelashes fluttered. "I canceled

the lease on our house. I tried to finish out the school year, but it was difficult. I ended up using the rest of my vacation time before giving my notice. Now that there's so much uncertainty with the baby, I'm taking life one day at a time."

Made sense. Continuing her day-to-day existence after losing Cam must have been hard.

"Casper is permanent, then?"

She pushed the meat around her plate. "I don't think in terms of *permanent* anymore."

He didn't, either.

Jackson Poff would turn over in his grave if he knew how poorly Wade had managed his inheritance. Wade never should have mortgaged JPX Ranch as collateral for the loan on Dudley Farms. If he sold the new property soon, even at a loss, he'd be able to pay off the loan and have his nest egg back in his bank account where it belonged. If he couldn't sell it…he'd have to put JPX Ranch up for sale, too.

Why had he been so careless with the land he loved? It had been pure arrogance to think he could add to his profits by buying a big farm when he only had experience growing hay.

"Do you have anyone who can help you?" he asked. "Cam's parents?"

"His mom died, and his dad and I aren't close." She patted her mouth with a napkin, but tension lines edged her lips.

"Friends?" He tried to think of who she'd had in her wedding, who she'd hung out with, but he drew a blank.

"Letting women into my life has never been my strong suit, Wade." She nudged her plate to the side and leaned back in the chair. "My life revolved around Cam and my job. I'm not like you. I don't even have to ask to know you're still best friends with Clint, Nash and Marshall."

It was true. They'd been his brothers since the day they'd met at Yearling Group Home for teen boys. He was blessed that two of them, at least, had settled into homes not far from his ranch. He could see them anytime he wanted.

Kit, for all appearances, was alone. He didn't like it. Who would take her to doctor's appointments? Who would make sure she got to the hospital when she went into labor? Who would hold her hand during the birth?

"You're not seriously thinking about having this baby all by yourself, are you?" The words tumbled out before he'd thought them through. "I mean, you need help. There's got to be someone who can take you to the hospital when you go into labor."

She flashed him a surprised glance, then averted her eyes. "Don't worry about it. I've got it covered."

"What does that mean?" He set his fork down. He'd lost his appetite, anyhow. "Do you have someone to be there with you or not?"

Her hands balled into fists, and she pulled them onto her lap.

"Kit?" He used his you'd-better-tell-me voice.

"I found an apartment two blocks away

from the hospital. It will be available in a month or so. And the extended-stay hotel is nearby, too. Like I said, I've got it covered."

That was her idea of having it covered? He wanted to wipe his hands down his cheeks in frustration.

"But what if—"

"My whole life is one big *what-if* right now, so please don't lecture me."

He clenched his jaw. Lecture her? He'd hound her until she talked sense. What did she think? That she could walk a few blocks to the hospital when she got contractions? Of all the foolish ideas...

"I'm doing what's best for me and the baby. Wyoming Medical Center has a level two neonatal intensive care unit, and, if necessary, they'll transfer the baby to a level three or level four NICU. I'm better off in Casper."

He couldn't argue with that. But more worries, more questions came to mind.

"You quit your job. What's your medical insurance situation?"

"I'm paying for an extension of the insurance I had through work."

"Can you afford it?"

"I have Cam's life insurance."

"Will it last?"

She glared at him. Wade didn't care. He needed to know she'd be all right.

"Honestly, I don't know. Specialists and hospitals tend to be expensive, even with insurance."

"If you need help..." He had no idea where he'd get the money, but if Kit was broke, he'd figure out something. Selling Del Poncho came to mind.

"I don't."

"Are you sure?" Why was he pressing her, when he wasn't in a position to help? Old habits died hard, he guessed.

She stared at him dead on. The muscle in her cheek flickered. "I'm not taking one red cent from you. This is my life, my baby and I'm a grown woman. I'll handle it. It's bad enough I had to ask you to let me stay here for the week."

What was that supposed to mean? Didn't she want his help? His friendship?

"You might want to sheath those claws. I thought we were friends."

"You're right. I'm sorry." She pinched the bridge of her nose. "I'm not good company lately. Thanks for dinner and everything. I think it's best if I get out of your hair." Pushing her chair back, she started to rise, and winced.

He was at her side in a heartbeat. "What's wrong? You okay? Is it the baby? Should I call the doctor?" Who was her doctor? Was there a baby doctor around here? He had no clue. His ranch was over thirty minutes to Sweet Dreams, not exactly ideal in an emergency, and Sweet Dreams didn't have a hospital.

"It's nothing." She patted his arm. "I get aches and pains now and then. They go away."

"I don't think you should be running around."

She let out a long-suffering sigh. "Do I

look like I'm running around? I got up from a chair."

"Why don't you sit on the couch? Kick those legs up. I'll put a movie on. Whatever you'd like."

With a sad smile, she shook her head. "Thanks, but I'm really tired. I think I'll go to bed. Don't feel like you have to cook for me and entertain me this week. I'll get along on my own just fine."

What if he didn't want her to get along on her own?

He'd done everything wrong tonight. He should do as she said and give her the space she needed. Tomorrow he had a meeting with Ray Simon, his real estate agent. The stack of bills he'd been hoarding in his home office meant he needed to come up with a plan.

He glanced at Kit. He'd try one more time.

"It's early," he said. "Stay."

"Like I said, I'm real tired."

He'd tried. It would have to be good enough.

"Then I guess I'll take you back."

* * *

Ten minutes later, Kit warred with her conscience as Wade parked his truck in front of her cabin. He'd been nothing but sweet and nice and caring since she'd arrived, and he'd offered to help with medical bills. Who did that? Only Wade. But she couldn't accept his money. Money always had strings attached, and she'd been tied up pretty tightly in the past. Never again.

Still…this was Wade, and she'd hurt his feelings, and he was the one person who knew her history. She could count on him, and she'd treated him poorly.

She needed—and wanted—to make it up to him.

"Wait, don't move a muscle. I'll come around and help you." Wade held his finger up, then got out and jogged over to her. His rough hand in her palm made her heart do a flip.

Strong, hardworking hands for a strong, hardworking man.

What would her life be like if she'd married someone like Wade instead of Cam?

What did it matter? No sense wasting energy on stupid thoughts like that. She'd made her bed and had to live with the consequences.

"Do you want to sit with me on the porch for a spell?" She gestured to the two rocking chairs angled to face the mountains.

"You sure?"

"Yeah, I'm sure."

The sun glowed low on the horizon as they settled into the chairs. A herd of cattle grazed in the distance. The rocking motion soothed her, and she wrapped her arms around her stomach. *Can you feel it, too, sweet one?* This might be the only time she got to rock her little boy.

Really, she had to stop being so morbid.

She'd enjoy the baby now and not think about the future.

Nagging at the back of her mind were the key moments that had triggered the losses in her life. Getting the belt on a daily basis before being sent to the first foster home as a five-year-old. Not being docile enough for the second family and moving to the next foster home. The third home was where she'd met Wade. Happiest days of her life. Until the family moved out of state, scattering the foster kids. The next place she'd earned her keep, tucked away her needs and emotions to ensure she had a place to live.

Being her real self never felt safe. Whenever her true feelings came out, bad things happened. Just look at Cam.

"Tell me about this place," she said. "I remember when you lived south of here. I'm assuming you still own that property. Is the little house still there?"

"The shack?" He clasped the ends of the rocker arms and slung one ankle over his knee. "I do still own it. That hundred acres was my first slice of owning a ranch. And, yeah, the shack is still there."

"It was hardly a shack. I liked it. It was cozy, cute."

"And infested with mice, lacking in insulation and tiny."

"It suited you." Her mood lightened at the memory of visiting him during one summer break. When she'd arrived, he'd been sweeping the floor, muttering about rodent droppings. He'd been younger, full of energy and ambition.

She peeked at his profile. Some things never changed. He was still full of energy and ambition.

When she was younger, she'd considered Wade her knight in shining armor. Still did. But he was all wrong for her. She'd known it then. She knew it now.

He was into building a ranch empire.

She was into raising a family.

The two concepts didn't gel where he was concerned. Ranching would always be his love, his priority. Kit had closed the door on any fantasy of being with him. Then she'd locked it, thrown away the key and bricked it over for good measure.

Wade was too attractive inside and out for her to revisit youthful fantasies.

How many times over the years had he told her he didn't see himself ever getting married?

Looking out over the land, she realized it had been years since she and Wade had really talked. After her wedding day, she'd felt it was inappropriate to keep texting and calling him, so they'd drifted apart, exchanging birthday cards and not much else.

She'd missed him. His friendship had been her lifeline until marrying Cam. And here Wade was extending his friendship again.

"I'm sorry, you know." She kept rocking.

"For what?"

"For not keeping in touch better."

He waved his hand dismissively. "Don't worry about that. Would have been weird with you being married and all."

Her chest grew tight. He understood. Most guys wouldn't have.

"Well, I'm sorry just the same. Why don't you fill me in on all I've missed? You were pretty tight-lipped about how you came to own this land. Do you own more, too? What have you been doing for the past couple of years?"

A shadow crossed his face and he narrowed his eyes as he stared off into the distance. "I always had my sights on this acreage, mainly because the man who owned it, Jackson Poff, didn't have kids to pass it down to. I figured it gave me a chance to negotiate, so I struck up a friendship with him."

"Wade!" She widened her eyes, tilting her head. "You used him?"

He flashed a grin. "No, Kitty Cat. I was up front with him from day one. I rolled up in my truck, introduced myself, told him I loved his land and planned on buying a portion of it someday. Then I offered to help him feed his cattle. He spat on the ground and told me to take a hike, but not in such friendly language."

She couldn't help it—she laughed.

"The next morning, I showed up again and

told him how I admired his pastures." He pointed to the right. "That section there to be precise. I asked him what his plans were for the day, and he told me he was checking fence and for me to take a hike—once more, not in such friendly language. I ignored him and helped him fix fence. For six months I came over every day after I'd taken care of my small cattle operation. And we became good friends. I told Jackson I wanted to buy some of the land when he retired."

"And he obviously retired." Her head rested against the back of the chair, and she relaxed for the first time in a long while. Wade's low, mellow voice soothed the rough places inside.

"No." He dropped his head. "I wish that's how it had gone."

"What happened?"

"He died. It was sudden."

Poor Wade. It sounded like he'd really enjoyed Jackson's company.

"And you bought this after he passed?"

He shook his head. "I would have. But I

didn't have to. He gave it to me. All of it. Almost eight thousand acres. The house, the cabins, the outbuildings, the cattle—everything. Even his substantial savings. I still can't believe it."

"Wow." She couldn't imagine anyone doing something so generous. "No one contested it?"

"Nope. Jackson didn't have any next of kin." His eyebrows furrowed. "He made everything possible for me. I likely never would have been able to afford to purchase this entire ranch. I'd hoped I could buy a slice of it—and I had no illusions about the fact I'd need a huge mortgage—but his generosity made it a moot point."

"So how much land do you own altogether, then?"

He told her about Dudley Farms, as well as a few smaller properties in the southern part of the state he rented out for pasture.

"I'm impressed." She savored a deep breath of the fresh air. The fact Wade's dream had come true warmed her soul. "You made it.

You did everything you said you were going to do."

"I haven't made it." He flashed her a confused glance. "Not by a long shot."

"What do you mean? You own thousands upon thousands of acres and run your own cow-calf operation here, as well." Wasn't all this enough for him? The thought of being responsible for so much land gave her a headache.

"Yeah, well, I put Dudley Farms up for sale."

"Why?"

"Doesn't matter." From his tone, she'd say he wasn't happy about it. "I hope it sells soon."

"If it doesn't?" The warmth of the air and the rocking motion made her eyelids heavy.

"It will."

"When will you have made it?" she asked lightly.

"What do you mean?"

"Well, I told you you'd made it, and you

said not by a long shot. How do you define making it?"

He didn't answer.

She yawned. He'd probably never be done acquiring properties. And since he hadn't married, she could confidently assume his conviction to stay single still held true. Exactly why she'd been wise to brick that wall over her heart all those years ago.

His priority was ranching. Her priority was her unborn child.

Exhaustion took over. She'd never been this tired in her life. She couldn't fight it any longer. She gave in to sleep.

Wade flipped pancakes the next morning in his kitchen. Tendrils of steam rose from his mug of coffee next to the griddle. The floor felt cool beneath his bare feet. Wearing athletic shorts and an old rodeo T-shirt from his friend Nash's bull-riding days, he inhaled the smell of batter and told himself for the eighteenth time that morning he'd done the right thing.

Earlier, he'd called his real estate agent and canceled his appointment. Ray had sounded shocked, and Wade didn't blame him. He couldn't remember the last time he'd backed out of an appointment.

*When will you have made it?*

Kit's question last night had caught him off guard. Then when she'd fallen asleep with her dark eyelashes fanned across her cheeks, he'd watched the gentle rise and fall of her chest, her hands still cradling her stomach as if she could keep the baby safe, and something had tumbled inside him.

She'd looked like the girl who'd grabbed his hand the day he'd arrived at the foster home where she'd been living. Full of excitement, she'd said, "Come on! I have something to show you!" And she'd dragged him through the never-ending backyard, past the sheds, beyond the horse pasture to a sliver of a creek. She'd crouched down, pointing at the water gurgling over the stones. "See them?"

"See what?" He'd crouched, too, somewhat mesmerized by her pretty green eyes and long brown hair pulled back in a ponytail. She was younger than him, but he'd instantly bonded with her. Probably because she was so full of life.

"There! The tadpoles. They're swimming!"

Black dots with skinny tails swirled in the water. The coolest thing he'd ever seen. Mostly because she'd been the one to show him.

What had happened to those days? Tadpoles and secrets and lemonade in Mrs. Bradley's kitchen.

The timer beeped. He flipped the pancakes. Browned to perfection. It was all in the timing.

The truth was he *had* made it. And, unfortunately, he was on the verge of losing it. But the appointment with Ray would have taken all morning, and he didn't want to leave Kit here on her own. Not yet. She'd barely touched her food last night. She was clearly exhausted. And there was a sharp edge to her he'd never seen. He didn't like thinking of her jaded about Cam dying and the baby's health problems. If he could soften that edge a bit, take care of her, make sure she ate and slept and relaxed, well, he'd cancel everything until she left next week.

His ranch manager could call in a few local teens to help out with the chores.

Just for the week, though.

Even thinking about not hustling out to check cattle tightened his chest uncomfortably.

It would be fine. Everyone took a vacation now and then.

Except him.

The smell of burning caught his attention. He lifted a pancake—black on one side. *Well, giddyap.* This was what happened when his mind wandered to unwelcome places. Perfectly good pancakes turned into hockey pucks. He tossed the ruined flapjacks in the trash and started a new batch.

Fifteen minutes later, he loaded the foil-covered platter of pancakes, a dish full of cooked bacon, strawberries, maple syrup, milk and orange juice into the back seat of his truck. Then he drove into the bright sunshine and headed to Kit's cabin.

After knocking several times, he contemplated his next move. Knock harder? Let her sleep?

Her pinched face when she'd gotten up from the table last night came to mind. What if something was wrong? She could be unconscious on the floor right this minute.

Pounding on the door, he yelled her name. If she didn't get out here in ten seconds, he was letting himself in.

He heard movement inside, and the relief almost buckled his knees. She opened the door, her hair mussed, eyes half-closed, and wearing a short-sleeved pajama top with matching shorts.

"What's wrong?" she asked.

A wave of embarrassment washed away his worry. What was wrong with him? He never overreacted. Why was he so worked up? He was worse than a nervous mama with a freshly born calf.

"Nothing." He tried to act cool. "I brought breakfast. Figured you were hungry."

"Really? Why all the noise?" She let him inside. "I'll be right back. Let me brush my teeth and get dressed."

As she walked away, he blew out a long exhalation. He had to stop fussing. By the time he'd brought in the food and set the table, he'd returned to normal.

"You made all this?" Kit appeared in a sundress. Her hair had been combed to fall over her shoulders, and her face, though pale, had more life to it than yesterday.

"I did." He hitched his thumb to the coffeemaker. "Should be done in a few minutes."

"Decaf?"

"Decaf? Why in the world would you want that? Might as well grind up the dirt out back to brew." He tore off two paper towels to use for napkins.

"The baby. I'm not supposed to have caffeine." She lifted the foil off the pancakes. "Oh, wow, this looks so delicious."

"I didn't realize about the coffee." He rubbed his chin. "I'll go into town later and get you some decaf."

"No, thanks. I can get my own food."

Stubborn as they came. But he knew how to work around her determination. He'd picked up a few secret weapons over the years.

"I'm going into town, anyway. You can either let me get you what you need or you can come with me. Your choice."

He held his breath, hoping she'd let him go alone and hoping even more she'd join him.

"We'll figure it out later."

And that was one of her secret weapons against him. The delay tactic.

"I'm surprised you aren't riding around the ranch. Or did you already check the cattle and do all your cowboy stuff?"

"Cowboy stuff?" He chuckled. "I figured I haven't seen you in a long while. I'll take a few days off."

She choked on her bacon, coughing. "You don't have to."

"I know."

"Seriously, Wade. I don't want to be a bother." She took a drink of milk. "Just do what you normally do."

"You won't be a bother. That's why I'm going to hang out with you. I miss you."

He didn't realize how much he meant it until he said it.

"Well, I'll ride into town with you then. But I insist you stick to your routine. I'll be boring to be around, anyhow. I've taken napping to a whole new level." She flashed him a half-hearted smile and averted her eyes.

She was lying. He knew her too well.

"You're sleeping pretty good, then?"

She nodded, shoving a big bite of pancake into her mouth.

He'd been right to take the time off. Kit wasn't sleeping. Her mind was probably racing in circles around the baby's health troubles. Or she was mourning Cam. Both, most likely.

He bit into a piece of bacon. Cam was gone, the baby had a hole in his heart and

Wade might not be able to fix any of it. But he could be present.

Kit needed a friend.

And, frankly, so did he.

It was only for a week. Nothing to worry about.

Then they'd go back to being long-distance friends. The way it should be.

Why didn't the thought fill him with relief?

Until he sold Dudley Farms and got his financial life back in order, he had to tread carefully.

# Chapter Three

A girl could live in a place like this forever. Kit sipped a glass of water on the porch of her cabin late Friday morning. The rocking chair had quickly become her favorite spot. She'd spent hours watching butterflies flit around and hawks circle overhead. The mountains added serenity to the scene. For the first time in years, she'd found space to breathe again. The anxieties of life didn't choke her here, and she'd been sleeping well, too.

She wouldn't get the results of the chromosome microarray tests for almost two more weeks, but she'd begun to make peace with whatever they might reveal. Every morning she prayed for her baby boy. Every evening, too.

Her cell phone rang. Probably Wade. Ever since she'd arrived three days ago, he insisted they eat most meals together. Afterward, she'd excuse herself to rest, and he'd wait precisely two hours to call and check on her. With anyone else it would be overbearing, but not with him.

He cared about her. Plain and simple.

The phone rang again, but she didn't recognize the number. "Hello?"

"Is this Kit McAllistor?"

"Speaking."

"This is Jambalaya Suites. A room opened up. You can check in after three this afternoon."

The extended-stay hotel. It would have been welcome news when she'd been driving to Wade's ranch, but after spending a few days here, she didn't immediately jump for joy at the chance to move on.

"Do you still want it?" The man sounded exasperated.

"Yes, thank you. I'll take it. I'll be there this afternoon."

After she hung up, she sighed, continuing to rock on the porch. She really didn't want to leave yet. But the longer she stayed, the harder it would be to go. She'd forgotten how calming the wide-open prairie could be.

Heaving herself to her feet, she cast a longing look at the countryside, then turned and went back into the cabin. She had to pack up her stuff. She'd stop in at the main house on her way out to thank Wade.

He'd be mad, of course, and maybe a little hurt she was leaving like this, but she couldn't face an argument right now. It was bad enough she'd be living in a hotel for weeks. The thought of being in a strange town and not knowing anyone didn't exactly sweeten the deal. Under no circumstances would the hotel room have a porch and butterflies and wildflowers and silence.

But she'd be close to the hospital. She

could start looking into job options for after the baby was born. Maybe she'd teach online classes. She'd figure out something.

After hoisting one of her suitcases onto the bed, she gathered her things. It didn't take long. A knock on the door came as she zipped her smallest bag. Her stomach clenched, and it wasn't because of the baby.

Wade wasn't going to be happy about her leaving like this.

"Come in," she hollered, rolling the luggage down the hall.

"What. Is. Going. On?" He stood in the living room, hands on his hips, legs wide and eyebrows furrowed.

"The hotel had an opening. I'm headed there in a little bit."

"No, you're not."

"Yes, I am."

"Nope." Embers licked to flames in his eyes. He pointed to her suitcase. "Roll that right back into the bedroom. You're staying here."

"I'm going to Casper. Today."

He pursed his lips, shaking his head. "I don't think that's a good idea."

"Well, I do." As much as she'd like to stay here indefinitely, she couldn't. She'd set her plans in motion, and if she changed them now, she might do something stupid. Like stay here and get too comfortable with the one man she could count on. The incredibly gorgeous, caring one who wasn't into love or marriage. She'd made many poor emotional decisions over the years, and she couldn't afford to make another one now. The baby had to come first.

His jaw could crack a walnut, and he opened his mouth, but she raised her hand. "You're not going to convince me, so don't bother trying." She resumed rolling the suitcase to the front door, but he blocked her path. Being within two feet of the strapping man rattled her. She glared at him. "Move."

"Make me."

Move that tall beam of solid steel? If she pushed him, she'd have to touch him, and touching him would merely remind her how appealing his strength was.

*"Wade!"* She almost stamped her foot.

"I don't like this. Casper is too far away, and you don't know anyone, and the hotel might have nasty bacteria and drifters."

Bacteria and drifters? Like she needed more to worry about at this point. "You're not my boss."

His expression softened. "No one's ever been the boss of you. I wouldn't want to be, and I'd never try."

Closing her eyes, she couldn't decide if it was an insult or a compliment. Either way, it solidified the truth—he viewed her as a friend. Same as she did him. And if she stayed, she'd be in danger of putting on those rose-colored glasses from her youth. She needed to concentrate on herself and the baby.

"Good," she said a little too briskly. "Then kindly put this suitcase in my trunk while I get the rest of my stuff."

A strained moment passed with neither of them speaking.

"Won't you consider it, at least?" He shrugged helplessly. "I think you should stay."

"This is best. For me. For the baby. And for you—you can get back to work. I know you've taken off a lot of time on account of me being here."

He exuded frustration. "Well, if you're dead set on going today, I'll drive you."

"No, I can't ask you to do that."

"You didn't. I offered."

Hours in the car with him? Her senses might not be able to take it.

"How would you get back?"

"I'd rent a car when we got there."

"Seems awfully complicated." She chewed her bottom lip. It would be nice not to have to drive, though.

"Really? Seems simple to me. Besides, I want to make sure this hotel is in a decent area. I don't want to worry about you getting mugged."

"I'm sure the location will be fine. I doubt I'd be in any kind of danger."

"You don't know that." He crossed his arms over his chest. "Either I drive you or you stay here. Those are the options."

"Or you move out of my way and I drive myself. I'm a big girl."

He had the grace to look sorry. "I know. It's not that I think you're incapable. It's just...well... I wouldn't be able to live with myself if something happened to you on the way there. Your car could break down. You could get a flat. Or what if you get pains or something?" He waved helplessly at her abdomen.

Why did he have to say the perfect thing? Her eyes prickled with emotion. Cam had barely spoken to her for months before he died. And the only reason she was pregnant was because of a last-ditch effort to save their marriage. Even if Cam had lived, her marriage would have ended. He'd been adamant about it.

To have a man care about her well-being like this was strange territory.

And she liked it.

But it was a mirage.

Wade cared about ranching and having lots of land. And he cared about her, too, because they were friends. That was all. She wasn't fooling herself into thinking he'd ever want more.

She didn't, either. But he had the power to tempt her.

Which meant she needed to get to Casper soon. Like today.

"Okay," she said. "You can drive me, but I'm staying in the hotel whether you find bacteria or drifters or not."

"We'll see about that."

Wade kept Kit's car below the speed limit. He wasn't in a hurry to deliver her. How could he keep an eye on her when she'd be living so far away? A honky-tonk song played on the radio. She was staring out her window. While they'd spent the first leg of the trip remembering old times, the past hour had been mostly quiet. As buildings dotted the side of the road more frequently, a sense of unease tightened his muscles. They were almost there.

And he wasn't ready for this time with her to end.

His phone's navigation system directed him through town. The closer they got to the address, the more danger signals flashed in his mind. It wasn't the older homes he minded, it was the fact they were run-down. He stopped at a traffic light and assessed the area. Graffiti marked a warehouse on the corner. A skinny dog without a collar ran by, and a group of three teen boys who spelled trouble sauntered down the sidewalk.

The light changed and he drove ahead, taking a left and pulling into the parking lot of Jambalaya Suites. The neighborhood around it clearly had taken a downturn in recent times. The exterior of the hotel was dated, and weeds poked through the lawn.

Kit didn't say a word. She got out of the car and slung her purse over her shoulder.

He fell in beside her as they strolled toward the entrance. A train whistle blared, practically deafening him, and Kit jumped, slapping her hand against her chest. He met her shocked gaze. "Wasn't expecting that."

"Me, neither." She raised her eyebrows. "Home sweet home."

Over his dead body…

They entered the lobby, and Wade forced himself to keep his cool. The forest green carpeting had stains and worn patches. Striped wallpaper peeled in several places. As they approached the front desk, he clenched and unclenched his hands and did everything in his power to stay quiet. The counter had deep scratch marks. Had someone knifed it? And what, for the love of Wyoming, was that smell?

*Breathe through your mouth.*

The clerk behind the desk didn't look up.

They waited.

And waited.

As much as he wanted to scoop Kit into his arms and run out of here, he remained silent. If he said one wrong thing, she'd dig her heels in. He *would* convince her not to stay here, but in order to do that, he needed a level of patience he might not possess.

"Excuse me." Kit's pleasant voice didn't fit here. *She* didn't belong here.

"Just a sec." The clerk continued to stare at the computer screen.

*Just a sec?* Wade was *this* close to grabbing the guy by the collar and informing him what good service entailed.

"Yeah?" Bored eyes looked up at them.

"Kit McAllistor." She lifted her chin. "You have a room for me."

"Oh, right."

"She'd like to see the room before she puts down a deposit." Wade leaned forward.

"Whatever you say." The clerk ignored them as he typed. Then he held out a key card to her. "Your room is on the second floor. End of the hall, Kate."

"It's Kit," Wade practically growled.

"Okay, *Kit*."

*Don't beat the twerp up. Keep your eyes on the prize.*

He'd have Kit in and out of here in ten minutes. Tops.

"Where are the elevators?" she asked the clerk.

"Don't have them. Stairs are to the left."

Wade held his arm out to her and gave the jerk the most lethal glare he could muster, but the kid had already resumed staring at the computer screen.

The smell of wet dog, mold, and what he could only describe as liver and onions filled the hall. Surely, the scent alone would send Kit running back to her car. She couldn't seriously be considering living here, could she?

They climbed the stairs and turned left. This hall smelled marginally better than the one downstairs. Kit stopped in front of the door. It looked like she was praying, but he couldn't be sure. Then she slid the card into the slot. Red light. She swiped it again. Red light.

He took it from her and quickly swiped it twice, getting a green light. She opened the door and walked in, with him on her heels.

The train whistle blew again, and the rumble of the cars moving on the tracks was so loud they could have been right outside the building. Wade crossed over to the window. The train *was* right outside the building. The railroad tracks butted up to the property. He swiped the curtains shut.

He could stay silent no longer.

He was getting her out of here.

Turning, he opened his mouth to let her know in no uncertain terms that this place was a dump and there was no way he was leaving her, but he didn't have a chance to speak.

With her hands over her face and her shoulders shaking, Kit sobbed.

*Stupid Jambalaya Suites.* Muttering under his breath, he took three strides and pulled her into his arms.

"It's okay, Kitty Cat," he said softly. "You're not staying here."

She lowered her hands, tears streaming down her face.

"I'm sorry, Wade, I don't mean to be like this. But the thought of spending the next month or so here... I'm already nauseous from the smell—and I can't take the noise and the carpet and the awful bedspread..."

"I know. I think someone heated up liver and onions, and that's unacceptable."

"I could handle the smell. I think I could, at least, but it's so loud, and there's no front porch with a rocker. And the bathroom tile freaks me out. Where are the butterflies? I can't do this!"

He didn't know what she was talking about, but if it meant she was coming home with him, he liked it. Keeping his arms around her, he stroked her hair. Soft, lush hair. "Shh... I know. This is no place for you."

"I agree." She stepped out of his embrace, tilting her chin up. "I'm finding another hotel."

"What?" Didn't she get it? She wasn't

staying in Casper in a hotel. She was coming back to JPX Ranch, where she'd have rest and fresh air and good food. And him.

He needed to keep an eye on her...as long as possible.

"Come on." She hurried to the door. "I'm serious. We have to find another hotel. Today."

The familiar no-budging tone had him gritting his teeth. Just when he thought he'd won, she threw down a new gauntlet. He couldn't argue with that tone. No one could.

"Fine." He'd take her to other hotels, but he wasn't going to leave her at any of them.

He hadn't been in the habit of praying for a long time. But he needed help. This was a situation he couldn't control on his own. Would God even listen to a guy like him? He knew he was saved. Believed Jesus had died and risen for him. But he hadn't been to church in years. And he kept a Bible in his nightstand only because when he left it on top all it did was gather dust.

*Look, God, I know we're not exactly tight,*

*but Kit's a praying woman. She might think she's better off here in Casper, but I need You to convince her to come back with me. I don't want her alone in her condition.*

Wade followed Kit out of the room. He clearly needed to work on his praying skills.

In the meantime, maybe if he gave her more reasons to come back with him, she'd cave. He'd think of them while they drove.

She hadn't felt this low in, well, a week, but today had been extra discouraging. Kit slid into the booth of the restaurant Wade had picked out. Her carefully constructed plan had fallen apart.

The best hotel with long-term vacancy was three times the price of Jambalaya Suites. She couldn't afford it, and even if she could, the room had been small, and she hadn't liked the location.

None of the rooms she'd toured today had a view of meadows. None of them had a big comfy bed and a gourmet kitchen. She'd felt claustrophobic in them. All the anxieties she'd been fighting a week ago had flooded back to her as she'd stood in the confined spaces.

If she stayed in any of the hotels, she'd spend every waking minute worrying about the baby. At Wade's she'd been able to rest, to think, to clear her head. And while she hadn't exactly been happy, she'd felt more like herself than she had in years. Which in itself unsettled her. Who was she if not Kit McAllistor?

"What are you hungry for?" Wade peered over his menu. "I'm starving. Let's get an appetizer."

She realized how hungry she was. "Yeah, I'm famished."

"I'll get us a sampler platter."

Sounded delicious. But food wasn't the main issue on her mind.

She wanted to go back to Wade's ranch. Just until the apartment opened up.

How could she ask that of him when he'd already driven her all the way here and she'd forced him to trek to hotel after hotel? He might not even want her staying in his cabin anymore. She was too much trouble for him. Just like she'd been for Cam.

She let out a loud sigh.

"What's wrong?" He folded the menu and placed it on the table.

"Nothing."

"I know better. That sound was not nothing."

"I guess I'm disappointed." She set her menu on top of his. "I thought this would be the perfect solution."

His eyebrows formed a V as he nodded.

"And the only hotel I'm considering is the last one we visited."

"The room was small."

"I don't need much space." It was true. She didn't. But it didn't have the porch and the view she'd enjoyed all week.

"Listen, I've been thinking." He leaned forward, clasping his hands and resting his forearms on the table. His baby blues captured hers. A girl could get lost for days in those eyes. "I know you want to be close to the hospital. But you're not due for months. Sweet Dreams has a medical clinic. I'm sure they have a baby doctor. And if they don't, any of the other neighboring towns must have at least one among them."

She could see where he was going with this, and the gesture was so wonderful, she almost started to cry again.

"I think you should put the hotel idea on hold for now. Just stay in my cabin. You liked it there. I could tell. You look more rested, and your color's back. It's good for the baby."

A lump grew in her throat, and she ducked her chin to keep a lid on her emotions.

"You want what's best for the little guy. The air, the rest, the peace of my land does you good. And if it does you good, then it's surely doing the baby good, too."

Her thoughts exactly. The fact he was being so tender with her when she knew he'd itched to take charge all day made her feel small. He'd been amazing from the minute she arrived on his ranch, and here he was, sacrificing his time to give her the support she needed.

"I don't know what to say, Wade. Thank you. I was trying to figure out how to tell you I wanted to come back with you, but I feel so bad about wasting your time."

"You aren't wasting my time. I needed to be here."

Kit regarded him thoughtfully. She'd never forgotten what he'd told her about his mother disappearing years ago. Maybe he was worried the same thing would happen to Kit.

"I will be all right on my own, you know," she said gently. "I would have been alone no matter what. The day I found out I was pregnant was the day Cam died."

"Oh." He blinked.

"He wanted a divorce, and I thought the baby would change his mind. When it didn't, I screamed things at him, terrible, awful things."

The way his mouth dropped open, she guessed he was trying to process everything.

"I'm the reason Cam is dead."

"That's crazy," he said. "He had a heart attack."

"Because of me. I've never lost control like that. I yelled the most hateful things… He slammed out the door. And had a heart attack a few hours later."

"Kit…you weren't responsible—"

"Yes, I was. He would not have had the heart attack if I hadn't been so angry. I would take back every horrible thing I said if I could."

"We all get angry. We all yell nasty things."

"I shouldn't have done it. I knew better." She felt steady now. She could see it all clearly. "The girl you grew up with doesn't exist anymore. She might not have ever existed."

"The Kit I grew up with is sitting right in front of me." His eyes blazed with intensity. "You didn't kill your husband."

"Only you would say that. You always saw the best in me. But I'm asking you not to. See the real me. No illusions."

"I see the real you. I wonder if you do." The words were quiet, sincere. "I'm taking you home."

*Home.* The word swamped her with relief. Maybe Wade didn't get it, but right now she didn't care.

"You'll see things more clearly when you've had some time to rest and move forward. And I don't care what you say or how you try to convince me you're some horrible person. You're not."

Some of the bricks she'd mortared over her heart tumbled down, but there wasn't much she could do about it now. The man sitting before her would be terribly easy to fall in love with.

And then she'd be right back to square one.

Every time she gave her heart away, eventually it was tossed back to her, bloody and damaged.

"And before we head back, we're driving to the apartment of yours to make sure it's in a safe location." He picked his menu back up. "Don't argue with me. It's nonnegotiable."

She'd just have to get another pile of bricks.

Living on his ranch for another month would be worth it.

# Chapter Four

Score one for team Croft. He'd gotten Kit
to give up on her foolish notion of staying
in some stinky, sketchy hotel. Wade zipped
Kit's car through the streets of Casper to
check out the apartment before they headed
back to the ranch. If the place wasn't up to
his standards, he'd get her to give up on that,
too.

And then what?

He couldn't ask her to stay on his ranch
forever. He might not even have a ranch in
the near future.

He had to stop thinking in worst-case scenarios. There was no way he was losing JPX

Ranch. Not after Jackson had entrusted him with it. He'd find a way to keep it going one way or another.

But none of that mattered at the moment. He was here for Kit. He still didn't get why she blamed herself for Cam's heart attack. Couldn't she see how irrational she was being?

The navigation system alerted him to take a left. He drove slowly until they found the apartment's address. The neighborhood left a lot to be desired. He ground his teeth together. Had she deliberately chosen the worst possible housing options? He pulled up to the curb in front of the building and kept the engine idling.

From the looks of it, the old brick building contained eight apartments, four in the front and four in the back. A metal set of stairs led to a narrow balcony with entrances to two apartments on the second floor. A ripped trash bag spilled its contents on the cement near one of the first-floor doors. Loud music could be heard thumping even from inside

Kit's car. An unshaven man smoked as he sat on top of an overturned five-gallon bucket. A slim woman with a toddler on her hip stood in an open doorway as she shouted at someone inside. Then she slammed the door shut, shifted the child to her other hip and kicked a canister of chewing tobacco out of the way. It rolled off the landing and fell to the grass.

"Well, this isn't what I expected." Kit's weak voice was so unlike her, he glanced her way. Yep, she looked green. Funny, since the scene before him made him see only red. The area looked eerily similar to the one where he'd lived with his mother as a small child.

"No big deal," he said gruffly. "You can keep on looking."

"The pictures online were much nicer."

"I don't doubt it."

"I should have known it was too good to be true. Cheap rent. Close to the hospital. Two bedrooms. Furnished." She gazed up momentarily. "It's okay. I'll make it work."

"You're kidding, right? This isn't the place for you. You tried, but you couldn't have known the apartment would be…" A pit. A cesspool. He didn't know how to finish the sentence without offending her.

"Go ahead and say it. It's a dive." She rubbed her temples.

And now he felt like a jerk. It wasn't like he wanted her to be miserable. He just couldn't wrap his head around her living here. The dude smoking on the overturned bucket didn't exactly look like the helpful, neighborly type.

Wade could just make out the pulse in the vein in her forehead. The only way he could in good conscience be okay with her moving to Casper alone was if she was in a safe, clean apartment. With a bodyguard posted out front at all times. Okay, the bodyguard was over the top, but, considering how his mother's life had ended, justified.

"Why don't we drive around and look at some other areas? Do an online search for a few other apartments, and we'll see if they look respectable."

"No. This will be fine."

"It's not fine. You living here isn't happening." Shifting into Drive, he checked his mirrors and merged back onto the road.

"I already put down the first and last months' rent. Most landlords won't rent to me since I don't have a job."

As her situation sank in, he couldn't help but press harder on the accelerator. A year ago, he would have paid the rent himself. He'd had more financial assets than he'd ever thought possible. And now he could only sit by and watch helplessly as Kit slogged through a bad situation.

"Stay on my ranch until the baby is born."

"You mean it, don't you?"

"Of course, Kitty Cat." He scoffed. "We're family."

Her head dipped too quickly. Had he made her cry again?

"I have to be close to the hospital, or I'd be tempted to take you up on your offer."

"Call the landlord and see if you can get your deposit back. We'll find you another place."

"I don't think he'll give me my deposit back."

"You can try. And right now I think we should look at a few other apartments in the area. Just in case."

"It's pointless. Like I said, without a job, no one is willing to rent to me."

"It won't hurt to look." If he sold Dudley Farms for close to what he was asking for it, he'd be in a position to help Kit out with the rent.

"Not tonight."

"It's almost dark, anyhow. We can head back. Why don't you try to rest?" He turned around to get to the main drag.

"Okay." Her shoulders sagged, and her head dropped back to the headrest. "Thanks, Wade."

"Don't mention it."

"I mean it. I appreciate everything you did today. Driving me here, carting me around to all the hotels, buying me dinner and helping me check out the apartment. I haven't had someone to rely on in a long time."

While his masculine pride swelled, his mind tripped over the last part. What about Cam? Hadn't she relied on him? Part of him wanted to ask, but the other part figured it was better not to know.

He'd spent years assuming Cam was the man of her dreams, that Cam was taking care of her and loving her and being the husband Wade could never be.

Maybe he'd been wrong.

Why had Cam wanted a divorce?

Wade peeked at Kit. Her eyelids had closed, but he could tell she wasn't sleeping. Just resting. She looked peaceful. The most content she'd appeared all day.

His questions could wait. If he started digging into her past, he might not like what he'd find. And the feelings he'd destroyed the day she'd gotten engaged could come back to bite him.

He had nothing to offer Kit at this point.

She needed someone who could support her and her baby boy. He'd never supported anyone but himself. Even if he got his finances back on track, he wasn't in a position to offer Kit much emotionally.

Sometimes loved ones disappeared, like his mother had, leaving despair and questions behind. And later he'd found out his worst fears had been realized. His mother had been kidnapped. Murdered.

It was better not to get too attached to anyone.

As the car drew farther away from civilization, he tried to brush off his anxieties.

If he could get his finances back in order, he'd be able to make sure Kit lived in a safe area and had the medical care the baby needed.

It was time to put JPX Ranch up for sale. He just had to make sure Kit and his friends didn't know about it.

He might have to give up his properties, but he wasn't about to give up his pride.

* * *

Kit woke to sunshine streaming in her room and the white comforter cocooning her in its soft nest. She glanced at the clock. After eleven. She couldn't remember the last time she'd slept so hard and for so long. Must be the country air.

Propping another pillow under her head, she luxuriated in the sensation of lingering in bed. A few hours of doing nothing sounded great. Especially now that she knew she'd be staying here longer—at least a few weeks. Maybe more.

She mentally came up with a plan for the day. She really should make sure there was a clinic nearby in case complications cropped up while she was here. She'd already been referred to a cardiologist and an obstetrician in Casper, but her appointments with them weren't until next month.

She was almost twenty-three weeks pregnant, and she still hadn't felt the baby kick.

Was the baby still alive?

Her lungs clenched. What if his little heart

had given out? She could be sitting here making all these plans, hoping for her son to live...

Lunging for her phone, she ignored the notifications and went straight to the internet to check the pregnancy websites she'd bookmarked. Her nerves ratcheted as her finger swiped through the ones about miscarriage.

Cramping, bleeding, dizziness, fever—she had none of the symptoms.

*Lord, thank You.*

She had to believe her son was growing. Every day—every minute—felt precious.

Resting against the pillows, she let her mind wander. Would the baby look like Cam? She wouldn't mind. She'd loved her husband once upon a time, but she wasn't mourning him. In some ways, she'd mourned him during their marriage. He'd disconnected from her long ago, and, after the funeral, she'd quickly adjusted to the concept that the marriage was truly over. He hadn't been around much while they were married, anyhow. She'd liked to stay home, and he'd made it clear that his nights with the boys were not to be missed.

Only those nights with the boys had turned into nights with the girls, too.

She'd been devastated when she found out about the first affair. He'd promised he'd made a mistake and that he would change. She'd believed him. But he'd continued to go out constantly, shutting her out of his life. After the second affair, her heart had started the process of mourning her dreams of happy-ever-after.

She'd accepted it. Put up with it.

Finding out about the baby had sparked hope in her, and she'd taken the pregnancy as a sign their marriage could be saved. She hadn't known he'd grown so close to a new girlfriend, close enough to want a divorce so he could marry the woman.

It did hurt that he'd never know his child. He'd been adamant he wasn't going to be in the baby's life, but if Cam had lived, he might have changed his mind.

*Are you really deluding yourself into thinking Cam would have embraced this baby?*

She could handle special needs and a hole in the heart and whatever complications got thrown her child's way. What about the rest of the world? If her baby did have Down syndrome, would they treat him differently as he grew older? Would she have to protect him from mean kids? Would she have to take care of him as an adult?

A fiery burst of heartburn hit her hard.

She was better off not dwelling on what-ifs and could-have-would-have-should-haves. She'd spent enough time doing that after moving to each new foster home. It changed nothing.

Swinging her legs over the bed, she stood, cradling her belly with one hand. Her phone showed two missed calls and a text. Sandra Bixby, one of the teachers she used to work with, had called and left a voice mail. The other number was probably a telemarketer. Her finger hovered over the voice mail button, but she decided to wait. She couldn't take a sympathetic message asking how she was doing, even if Sandra had always been kind to her.

Kit had never opened up about her personal life with her coworkers. How many times in high school had she confided something to a girlfriend, only to have her pain gossiped about and mocked? It had been bad enough not having a real family to live with. By the time she got to college, she'd learned to keep her private life close to her heart.

Kit hadn't told anyone except Wade about the baby's health problems. He was also the only one who knew she'd been having marriage issues—well, besides the two women Cam had cheated with, as well as the one he'd claimed he was going to marry.

Wade texted her. He was riding out with his ranch manager and wouldn't be back until supper. Which reminded her...she was starving.

Listening to Sandra's phone message could wait. Breakfast—scratch that, lunch—could not.

If Wade was out working, maybe she could

repay him in a tiny way for all he'd done for her this week. She'd cook him a hearty meal even a cowboy couldn't turn down. But her supplies were slim here.

She texted him. I'll cook supper. Do you mind if I raid your cupboards?

Her phone rang. Well, that was quick.

"Hello?"

"Kit?"

Sandra. Her stomach grew twirly. Why hadn't she checked the caller? "Yes?"

"It's Sandra. How are you holding up?"

Like four-week-old celery in the hot sun. "I'm okay."

"I stopped by your house the other day to drop off some baby supplies, but there was a For Rent sign out front and no one answered. Did you move?"

*Here we go. Questions I don't want to answer.*

"I'm staying with a friend for a while."

"But you'll be coming back?"

Closing her eyes, she fought for the right words. What was the appropriate response?

She'd never been good at this. Didn't want to open her mouth and have every skeleton in her closet topple out.

"Um, no. I'm moving to Casper."

"Casper? Did you get a new job or something?"

Emotion pressed against the backs of her eyes. How she wished she was moving for something as hopeful as a new job.

"Not exactly. Life's been…well, it's been rough lately."

"I can't imagine what you're going through." Sandra's voice filled with sympathy. "Losing Cam. You two always seemed like the perfect couple. And the baby…he would have loved your child. I'm so sorry you'll have to raise the baby without him. If there's anything I can do to help…"

And this was why she should have checked her phone before answering it. Everything inside her wanted to scream that they weren't the perfect couple and that precious Cam hadn't even wanted the baby and wouldn't have loved it and how dare Sandra presume to make him out to be a good guy.

"Thanks, Sandra. I appreciate it." She tried not to choke on the words.

"If you give me an address, I'll send the baby things to you."

The kind gesture shrank Kit down to the size of a mouse. Sandra always had a pleasant word for her when they passed each other in the halls, and she'd organized funeral flowers from the school staff as well as dropped off casseroles twice. Maybe Kit had been wrong to lump her in with the girls who'd turned on her in the past.

"You don't have to do that."

"I want to. Don't tell me you already have everything for the baby. Trust me. You always need more."

Have everything for the baby?

She had nothing. Not one thing.

"I haven't exactly started shopping for infant items yet."

"Well, I figured as much, with all you've

been through. The other teachers contributed, too. I'll box all this up and ship it first thing."

Kit didn't know if she could handle opening a box of baby delights. It would make it all the more devastating if her son died.

She just wouldn't open the box.

"I'll send you the address."

"Be sure you do, or I'll hound you for it."

"I promise. I'll text it to you as soon as we hang up."

"Okay. Take care of yourself, you hear? I'm praying for you."

Praying for her… Kit closed her eyes. Sadness and gratitude clogged her throat. "I need those prayers. Thank you."

She hung up. Before Kit could change her mind, she quickly texted Sandra the address of Wade's ranch. Then she headed to the kitchen to fix herself some food.

At some point she needed to buy baby supplies.

If the sweet child would just kick, make his presence known somehow, it would be easier to move forward. The days were ticking down until she'd find out if he'd be dealing with more than a hole in his heart.

Her phone chimed. Wade texted her. Raid away. My cupboards are your cupboards if you're cooking.

One kind deed deserved another. She'd make a good meal for Wade. And she'd come up with a way to thank Sandra for all she'd done. And maybe, just maybe, she'd forget about the baby's problems and enjoy the moment for once.

He had to stop fretting about Kit. Wade pulled on a clean pair of jeans after showering. The aroma of garlic and cheese hit him hard. When he'd walked into his house twenty minutes ago after a long day of riding the ranch, the first thing he'd seen was Kit tossing a salad. She'd cheerfully announced the lasagna would be done in half an hour. The scene had affected him a little too much. He'd practically sprinted down the hall to his master suite.

How was he supposed to concentrate on

the ranch, the bills and Dudley Farms languishing away when his brain was filled with concern for Kit's future?

And then, to walk into his home—which normally was silent, dark and smelled like leather—and have every one of his senses flame to life because of her?

It wouldn't do.

As much as he pooh-poohed his friends' domesticity, he could easily be sucked into fantasies about it if it meant piping hot lasagna and Kit smiling away.

He yanked the T-shirt over his head and shoved his arms into it. This was ridiculous. He'd ridden around the ranch for hours, helped move cattle and left a message for Ray earlier. He'd done what he needed to do.

So why was he so keyed up to eat dinner?

He braced his hands on the edge of the bathroom counter and stared at his reflection in the mirror. *Get yourself together, man. You're too old to act like this. And don't go out there being all weird. Treat her like you normally do.*

After taking a deep breath and running the towel over his damp hair one more time, he padded into the kitchen. Kit was pulling the lasagna out of the oven. His heart skipped two beats.

*Act normal.*

"All this for me? I hope you're not hungry." He winked at her and noticed the table had been set. "What's left for me to do?"

"Well, I plan on eating, too." She smiled. "You can sit down. It's ready."

"Here, let me." He took the oven mitts from her and carried the steaming dish to the table while she brought over the salad. "So what did you do all day while I worked my fingers to the bone on the ranch?"

That brought a smile. Her cheeks grew pink. "Your fingers look fine to me. In fact, they look mighty delicate. Not a callus to be seen."

"I'll have you know these are hardworking hands." He held them up and wiggled his fingers.

"Uh-huh." She slid a large slice of lasagna onto his plate. The cheese oozed down the sides. "Well, while you were doing your cowboy things, one of the teachers I used to work with called."

*Cowboy things.* Her phrase made him smile. "Oh, yeah?"

"She's sending me some baby supplies. I gave her your address. If a box comes for me, you'll know why."

Speaking of baby supplies… "Do you have what you need for the little guy?"

She averted her gaze, shaking her head.

"When are you supposed to start shopping for that stuff?" He cut off a bite of lasagna with his fork. Looked hot enough to melt iron. He'd let it cool a minute. His mind began swimming with items babies needed. Diapers. Bottles. A bed. Clothes. And more. Lots more. But what? He wouldn't know where to begin. "What do babies need?"

She finished chewing a bite of bread. "I'm not sure, but I've got time to figure it out."

Early October, she'd said. It gave her—

he mentally ticked off weeks—right around four months. Plenty of time. Or was it?

"I guess you can see what your friend sends and go from there."

"I guess."

He glanced at her. "Don't sound so enthusiastic."

Guilt flashed across her face. "It might be better if I shop after I get settled in Casper. Easier than moving it all, you know."

"I've got a big truck. Shop away. We'll get it there."

She didn't reply, just took a bite of her salad. Why wasn't she jumping all over buying the baby items? Did she think she could bring the baby home without having a crib and diapers and whatnot?

"Don't you want to be prepared?" he asked.

She stretched her neck to the side, looking like she'd rather be anywhere but here. Maybe she didn't know what to purchase.

He tore off a hunk of garlic bread. "Lexi went out and bought the entire baby department of a store last month when she and Clint found out they were expecting. She could tell you what you need if you're not sure."

Her forehead wrinkled. "Who's Lexi?"

"Clint's wife. You remember Clint Romine?"

"I remember Clint. I didn't realize he'd gotten married and is expecting..." The words trailed off.

"Trust me, I was shocked when he told me he'd fallen in love. I mean, we're talking about Clint. You know how quiet he is. But he's taken to married life. So has Nash. He's raising his little sister—and when I say little, I'm talking five years old—and he got hitched, too."

"Sounds like love is in the air for your friends."

He nodded. "Even Marshall is taking the plunge. Next month. In three weeks, to be precise. I'm one of the groomsmen."

Her fork clattered to the table, and she

swiped it up, keeping her gaze on the food. Had he said something wrong?

"Okay, what's going on? You're acting funny." He leaned back in his chair and watched her. Her eyes wouldn't meet his.

"I'm happy for your friends. It's just hard knowing..." Her jaw shifted.

Well, he'd gone and put his foot in his mouth big-time. Here he was, jabbering on about his happily married friends and their families, while she had no husband and a baby with health issues. *Great going, Croft.*

"I'm sorry," he said. "Me and my big mouth."

"Don't say that." She swallowed. "It's just...well, I've been thinking I should have felt the baby kick by now."

The food in his stomach congealed. If the baby wasn't kicking... A wave of sadness at the thought of the boy not making it crashed over him.

"What are you saying? Do you think...?"

Her eyes were filled with anguish, but

she gave her head a little shake. "I think he's okay."

"How do you know?"

"I don't have the signs of a miscarriage. I'm not cramping or bleeding or anything."

He pushed his chair back. "Maybe I should take you to the hospital. You know, to be sure."

"The nearest hospital is too far away. I'm fine. Really. The baby was alive when I had all the testing. I just think too much. And thinking leads to worrying. I keep trying to leave it in God's hands where it belongs, but five seconds later, the anxieties mount."

Leaving it in God's hands sounded good, but how could she know if He'd come through for her? God hadn't come through for his mother.

"In fact, I know what I need. Tomorrow's Sunday. I'm going to church."

He'd officially lost his appetite. The last time he'd gone to church had been for Nash's wedding. Wade hadn't attended a regular service in years.

It was on the tip of his tongue to offer to take her. But church? Him?

His cell phone rang. Ray Simons, his real estate agent. *Please let this be good news.*

He lurched to his feet and answered it, padding away from the table down the hallway to his home office. "What have you got?"

"I heard through the grapevine there's a couple looking for a ranch with a lot of acreage. I already talked to their agent about Dudley Farms. Should I mention JPX Ranch as a possibility, too?"

His chest hurt. All the hours spent with Jackson, getting to know every rock, every gully, every inch of pasture had been like spending time with the father he'd never had. And then, when the lawyer called him after Jackson died, he'd found out he'd been given the ranch outright. All of it his! Along with Jackson's savings and other assets...

He'd squandered it. Hadn't treated it like the precious gem it was. His greed had put it and his future in jeopardy.

"Go ahead, but don't advertise it yet. We can discuss it more on Monday if you're free."

"Good. And, yeah, I'm free." His cheeriness sounded through the line loud and clear. "Don't change your mind, now. Buyers are in short supply. From the sound of it, your ranch is exactly what this couple is looking for."

His chest squeezed even more tightly. What if they bought JPX Ranch? Would he have to move to Dudley Farms?

He wasn't a farmer. He was a rancher.

Why had he risked everything he loved to try something he didn't know much about?

"I understand."

"I'll call you if I hear anything," Ray said. "See you Monday."

"See you then." He tapped his index finger against the back of the phone as he returned to the table.

"Is everything all right?" Kit's clear gaze kicked him right in the chest.

Less than two minutes. That's all it had taken for him to forget she was there.

He'd never considered himself husband material, and it didn't take a genius to see he'd been right. Over the years he'd done a good job of not getting too close to a woman. When he thought about his mother...well, he wasn't going through that again.

This anxiety about Kit felt familiar.

He slid back into his chair. "Everything's fine."

"Nice try." She arched her eyebrows. "I know when something is bothering you."

Why her words comforted him, he couldn't say. Maybe it was just nice to have someone know him well enough to care. He didn't want to shut her out. He also didn't want to tell her how he'd messed up.

"That was my real estate agent." He cut a bite of the lasagna, which, thankfully, was no longer burning a hole through his plate.

"Good news?" She smiled, then sipped her water.

"It might be. A couple is looking for acreage. I'm heading into town Monday afternoon to talk to him."

"I thought you were obsessed with buying land, not getting rid of it."

"Obsessed?" He glanced up and wished he hadn't. She was giving him the watchful probe. "Nah. I'm making some business decisions."

Time to change the subject. It wouldn't kill him to offer to take her to church. Chances were she'd insist on driving herself, anyhow. "Why don't I take you to church tomorrow?"

A few seconds ticked by as she continued to stare. Then her expression cleared. "I'd like that. What time should I be ready?"

He had no clue. A part of him hoped she'd tell him not to bother. "I'll find out."

"Thanks." She cocked her head to the side. "If you want to talk about whatever is going on, I'm here."

Nothing like a sharp poke to the ol' conscience. He couldn't talk to her about this—couldn't talk to anyone about it. Maybe someday, after he'd fixed the mess, he'd be able to share it as a life lesson. But until then…he was changing the subject.

"So today, I was out riding and I came across this mean mama cow. I've been tired of that broad for months. But she always has healthy calves, so I put up with her, you know?" He told her about the cattle on the ranch and how a section of fence needed to be replaced soon.

She laughed at the right places, but he had the feeling he'd disappointed her.

Well, she could join the club. He disappointed himself, too.

As the sun set, Kit rocked on her porch. Wade had dropped her off a few minutes ago. The lasagna had been a success. The dinner itself, though, had been disconcerting. Ever since she'd driven into JPX Ranch, she'd been lapping up the attention Wade lavished on her. When he'd taken the phone call right in the middle of their meal, it had been a wake-up call.

How many meals had she finished alone

because Cam had gotten a call from one of his buddies during it?

The interruption she could forgive, but something was bothering Wade, and he'd refused to confide in her.

That's what hurt.

She tried to focus on the orange and purple streaks feathering across the sky. Her heart wasn't in the sunset.

Maybe it was time to face facts. As a girl, she'd been tossed aside again and again. The message had been received—she was unimportant. In her marriage, she had been, too.

But she'd never felt unimportant with Wade.

Until tonight.

Oh, she wasn't being fair. When she needed him, he was her rock. Didn't change the facts, though.

Her home wasn't here.

After church tomorrow, she was looking into other apartments, and if she found a better one that would lease to her without her having a job, she'd call the landlord in

Casper about getting her deposit back. If not, she'd have to suck it up and live there until she had the baby and went back to work.

*Don't worry, baby. I'm going to be the best mom you could have. I'm putting you first. No one ever put me first, and I don't want that for you. I want you to know how loved you are. I'll do anything for you.*

Gently rubbing her tummy, she continued to rock.

*God, do You have a plan for me? I know You love me. Thank You for that, but is there more? If the baby dies, what do I do? What am I here for? Do I even matter?*

Everyone had a reason for being here. She trusted God would let her know her purpose in His time. She wasn't content with being unimportant anymore. She hadn't been content there in a long time.

# Chapter Five

Tempted to loosen his collar, Wade shifted in his seat on the pew the next morning. He'd been doing life on his own just fine since the day he legally became an adult. Sitting here, singing hymns and listening to the service—or trying to, anyway—reminded him he was no longer doing life fine on his own. He'd always tried to make the most of what he'd been given, which, admittedly, he'd failed at recently, but ever since last night, his conscience had been niggling him. Did he have his priorities all wrong?

He glanced Kit's way. Her sundress and long brown hair pulled into a braid made her appear younger than she was. She stared intently at the pulpit, and she looked peaceful, like she was soaking in the sermon.

Unlike him.

He stretched his neck from side to side. How could she sit there and hang on every word? The only words he could hang on to right now would be *Congratulations, you got an offer on Dudley Farms.*

That's what he'd been hoping to hear last night when he'd taken Ray's call in the middle of a meal with Kit.

That had been a jerk move.

He should have waited until they finished the meal and called Ray back. He could sense her distancing herself from him. Part of him was glad. Her seeing his true colors kept him safe. But the other part of him... didn't like those true colors as much as he used to. Sometimes he wanted to be a better man.

*A better man? Get ahold of yourself. This is what happens when you go to church.*

Another hymn started playing, and Kit's

voice rang off-key. What she lacked in musical talent she made up for with enthusiasm. He began to sing, too. The words were familiar, and as he started into the second verse, he remembered all the times he'd come to this very building as a teen with Dottie and Big Bob Lavert. They'd been in charge of Yearling Group Home, and they'd given him a real education. Taught him how to be a moral, upright citizen.

Was he a moral, upright citizen?

The words to the hymn stuck in his throat. How could he sing about needing God's strength when he relied solely on his own?

This was why he should have stayed home. He wouldn't be thinking about things he was better off leaving alone.

Kit's arm brushed his as they stood for the final prayer. A tingling sensation rushed over his skin. He tried not to let it affect him. He could see why she would need God's strength. There wasn't a thing she could do about the condition of the baby growing inside her.

But why would she find comfort in God? Why wasn't she mad at Him? Her husband had been ready to divorce her. Then the idiot had died, leaving her pregnant and alone. And the baby, who had a hole in his heart, might have special needs or might not even live.

Why wasn't she mad at God?

Wade would be.

Thankfully, the service ended and he escorted her from the pew. He hoped Kit was comforted by the service. If anyone deserved a happy ending, it was her.

He followed her out of the church and onto the lawn. A hand on his shoulder made him turn.

"Are you terminal or something? Since when do you go to church?" Nash Bolton stood next to him with his typical cocky grin. Then he turned to Kit and pretended to clutch his heart. "Say it isn't so—Kit? Is that you?"

She smiled, revealing a row of pretty white teeth. "It's good to see you, Nash."

Nash's wife, Amy, sidled up next to him as their little girl, Ruby, ran to Wade and lifted her arms for him to pick her up. "Uncle Wade!"

"My favorite cowgirl!" Wade hugged the tiny blonde close. She kissed his cheek before wriggling to be set back on her feet.

"You have to come over and see me ride Chantilly." Her eyes lit up.

"Name the time. I'll be there." He winked. He'd bought her the horse last year as a welcome home present when Nash took custody of her. Best gift he'd given to anyone in years. He loved spending time with Ruby. Although not related by blood, he considered himself her uncle, and she, his niece.

"Promise?"

"Would I lie to my favorite cowgirl?" That brought a smile to her face.

"Congratulations, I hear you got married." Kit smiled at Nash.

"I had to beg, but I got this incredible lady to agree." Nash put his arm around Amy's shoulders. "Amy, this is Kit McAllistor. She and Wade go way back. Kit, this is my wife, Amy, and our daughter, Ruby."

"It's nice to meet you." Kit shook Amy's hand and addressed Ruby. "Are you going to school yet?"

Ruby lifted wide blue-green eyes to her. "I'm all done with preschool. The teacher gave me a paper with my name on it and everything."

"That's wonderful."

"Mommy says real school will be fun." She bit her lower lip. "I don't know. It's awfully big."

"It might seem big now, but you'll know your way around in no time," Kit said. "And you're going to learn all kinds of neat stuff. I'm a teacher."

"Can I be in your class?" She clasped her hands together and stared up with hope.

Kit laughed, caressing her tummy. "I would love to have you in my class, but I'm taking a break from teaching so I can have a baby."

"A baby!" She looked about to burst, then she solemnly nodded. "Aunt Lexi is having a baby, too."

"Speaking of…" Clint and Lexi joined the group. "Howdy, Kit. This is my wife, Lexi. Lexi, Kit."

They exchanged hellos, but before they could continue the conversation, Nash raised his hand. "Let's take this to Dottie's Diner and catch up over some breakfast."

Wade leaned in to Kit. "Are you okay with that?"

"Fine with me." She turned to him, her face glowing.

"We'll meet you guys over there." Taking Kit's arm, he guided her toward the parking lot. He loved his friends. He loved breakfast. He really loved Dottie. But joining the gang with Kit felt an awful lot like getting initiated into a club he had no intention of becoming a member of.

The marriage club.

Marriage club. He scoffed. This was just a breakfast. Nothing more.

* * *

The diner's exuberant atmosphere infected Kit as platters of eggs, bacon and waffles arrived. She sat next to Wade. Lexi and Amy chatted next to each other across from her, and Ruby had claimed the chair beside Kit's. The men talked calves and bull riding on the other side of Wade. Church earlier had soothed her troubles, making her believe she'd be okay no matter what happened with the baby. And she hadn't had time to fret about meeting Clint's and Nash's wives, since it had happened naturally. Both Amy and Lexi seemed nice and accepting.

Would they be so accepting if they knew the truth about her marriage? And what about the reality of her baby's health? She couldn't handle a Q and A session about him right now. She didn't have it in her to tell them about the hole in his heart. But smiling and nodding had never been her style, either.

She thought of Sandra Bixby. The woman had gone out of her way to be nice to her. Kit was getting tired of keeping people at a distance. But she also didn't want to scare them away by burdening them with her problems.

Nash clanged a butter knife against his mug. "While we're all together, Amy and I have an announcement."

The rest of the diner continued to buzz with laughter and conversation, while everyone at their table looked expectantly at Nash. Kit sneaked a peek at Amy. Her cheeks glowed pink, and her brown eyes sparkled.

"We found out we're having a baby." Nash glanced over at Amy with a look full of tenderness. He positively beamed. The table erupted in a round of congratulations. Lexi actually started to cry.

Kit's heart squeezed at the obvious connection everyone felt. The love flowing between Nash and Amy had been what she'd hoped to have with Cam. He never would have announced their pregnancy to friends, but then, they didn't have many friends. She'd give about anything for a relationship like Nash and Amy's or Clint and Lexi's.

"I thought it was a secret, Daddy!" Ruby scolded.

"It was, RuRu. Just until today."

Ruby tugged on Kit's hand. "Is my mommy's tummy going to get round like yours?"

"Yes, it will." Her voice cracked. She sipped her orange juice and tried to appear as happy as everyone else.

"I hope Mommy has a girl. I want a sister."

"Well, I'm having a little boy." She smiled down at Ruby. The girl was too cute.

"You are? How can you tell?"

"The doctor has a special wand to take pictures of the baby. Some people like it to be a surprise, but I wanted to know what I'm having."

"I'm telling Mommy to go get pictures tomorrow. I want a special wand, too!"

Kit laughed. "She'll have to wait a few months before the doctor can tell if it's a boy or a girl, and only doctors can use the wand."

Ruby's face fell.

"Ruby, remember what we told you?"

Amy prodded gently. "We'll take whatever God gives us."

"Well, I'm praying for a sister." She hopped off her chair, went to Nash and climbed onto his lap.

"I'm a little anxious." Amy looked at Kit, then Lexi. "I'll feel better after the three-month mark. I've wanted a baby for so long. What if something goes wrong?"

Kit's throat felt scratchy. She wanted to re-assure her, but how could she? It would be cruel to burden her or Lexi, who was just starting to show with her own baby bump, with news about her son.

"I felt the same way, Amy." Lexi put her arm around her and leaned in for a side hug. "I still worry. What if I get in a car accident? What if the cord wraps around the baby's neck? What if… I have to tell myself to stop worrying."

Amy nodded. "I know you're right. From the minute we found out, though, I've flip-flopped between pure joy and pure fear."

Kit hadn't worried much about the baby

before finding out about the hole in his heart. She'd resided in pure bliss at the thought of having a child. Dealing with Cam's final words as well as his death had made her heart numb. The baby had been a welcome reprieve from reality. She'd done what she always had. Made the best of a bad situation.

That was what she was doing now, too, she supposed.

"When are you due, Kit?" Lexi asked.

"Beginning of October." Kit shook her thoughts away. "What about you?"

"My official date is December 4. My clothes already feel tight." Lexi puffed out her cheeks and widened her eyes. Then she turned to Amy. "When are you due?"

"End of January. Can you believe it? Our kids will practically be siblings."

Siblings. Kit's heart pinched. If her baby lived, he wouldn't have siblings.

Wade touched her hand. "Are you okay?"

His eyes swam with concern and questions.

"Yeah." Trying to smile, she nodded quickly.

"I'm fine. Excuse me a minute." She set her napkin down and pushed her chair back. Then she weaved through the packed diner toward the restroom.

Why did a simple breakfast have to be so complicated? She locked herself in a stall and realized her hands were shaking. Her emotions had been colliding ever since Nash announced Amy's pregnancy. And then Lexi's and Amy's honesty about their fears had made her want to join in and tell them the truth—she was terrified she'd lose her baby.

Tears welled in her eyes. Their babies would have fathers who adored them. Lexi and Amy had strong men who would comfort them and support them throughout the pregnancy. Neither woman had to worry about going into labor alone. Neither had to worry about her baby having special needs. Or living in a horrible apartment in a strange town.

One tear fell to her cheek, then another.

She swiped both away and patted her cheeks with toilet paper.

Pulling herself together, she splashed water on her face and left the bathroom. She took two steps and felt a hand on her shoulder.

"You feeling okay, sunshine?" Dottie Lavert pulled her aside.

"I'm fine, Dottie, thanks for asking." She'd met Dottie several times over the years and always smiled at Dottie's nickname for her. Sunshine. Lately, all she felt was gloom.

"You need to get off your feet and have one of my ooey-gooey cinnamon rolls. I'll bring one over to you in a jiffy. I sure am glad you're staying out at Wade's."

She was, too. "Thanks."

Dottie winked and sauntered toward the kitchen. Kit returned to the table as Lexi was speaking to Amy. "Dr. Landor used to work with high-risk pregnancies in Chicago. I'm so glad she started a practice here."

"Can you give me her number?" Amy asked.

"Of course. She's taking new patients, too.

She's a newlywed, and her husband grew up in Sweet Dreams, so they decided to relocate."

An obstetrician who had experience with high-risk pregnancies? At least there was help nearby if anything were to go wrong before she moved to Casper.

In the midst of suffering, God always provided mercy.

*Thank You, Lord.*

She'd take the good with the bad. And be thankful for any crumb of hope.

Wade hiked back from the stables to his house. After breakfast, he'd dropped Kit off at her cabin, saddled up his favorite quarter horse, Thunder, and ridden around the ranch. The ground was dry and hard, and wisps of clouds streaked overhead. He'd come across a prairie dog family, a doe with twin fawns and three elk. He loved the rugged land and all its occupants—well, except for rattlers. He could do without those. There was something about this slice of Wyoming that cleared his head and made him feel like he belonged in the world.

But being out here hammered home the fact he might lose it. It was time to tally the stack of bills he'd been avoiding.

Taking long strides, he cast a quick glance at the cabins down the lane. Kit wasn't on her porch. She must be resting.

This morning at the diner Kit had seemed to enjoy breakfast with his friends. But then he'd noticed she'd grown quiet. And pale. And just like that, his gut had clenched and his mind had raced with worries.

Was she all right? Really all right? And would she tell him if she wasn't?

He'd been blindsided so many times as a kid. Zipping along, thinking everything was stable, and then he'd get moved to another home. When he and Kit had been separated, he'd changed. Grown resentful. His mood had hardened. It was a good thing he'd been placed at Yearling. Big Bob and Dottie had helped smooth him out again.

He still feared getting ripped away from

loved ones. He could admit it. But it was hard not to notice that all the creatures he'd encountered today, including his friends, had someone to share life with.

He entered through the sliding doors off the patio and headed straight to his bedroom to change. After slipping into fresh jeans and a T-shirt, he walked to the other side of his home where his office was located. On the way down the hall he glanced into the guest rooms. The room across from the office made him pause. It would make a nice nursery—a guest nursery—for Kit and the baby if they wanted to visit.

A text dinged. Would you be mad if I used your supplies to bake cookies?

Cookies? Who got mad about those? He texted her back. Not if you let me have some of the dough.

Two seconds passed. One bite. That's all. I know you.

He laughed and replied, When do you want me to come get you?

A knock from the patio door had him hurrying to the living room. Kit stood outside. She still wore the simple sundress from earlier. She grinned.

"I would have picked you up." He slid open the door and escorted her inside. "You shouldn't be walking so far."

"It's not far. Exercise is good for me and the baby."

He followed her to the kitchen. "What if you turn your ankle or something?"

"I'm not going to turn an ankle." She bent to poke through his cupboards.

"I don't like you traipsing about."

"Traipsing?" Her laugh tinkled. "I can handle the walk."

He studied her through narrowed eyes. She looked better than she had at the diner. There was a glow about her, and he was happy to see her cheeks weren't as sunken as they'd been when she'd arrived. Maybe it was due to her smile.

"What can I do?" He thumped his knuckles on the countertop.

"Thaw out some butter. I need two sticks."

He opened his fridge and found the butter. "It's going to take a long time to thaw."

"Pop them in a bowl in the microwave for twenty seconds."

He tossed both sticks in a bowl. "Won't they blow up?"

"You have to take the paper off first, you goofball, and no, they won't blow up. Unless you put them in for several minutes or something."

"Well, now you tell me." He winked at her. Then he unpeeled the wax paper from each stick and put them in the microwave. The bills had waited this long. They could wait a few hours more.

Kit found the sugar and flour. She started pouring ingredients in a large bowl.

"Can you grab two eggs for me?" she called over her shoulder as he removed the butter from the microwave.

"Sure thing." He set them next to the bowl. Then he rounded the counter, sat on a stool and watched her mix everything together. She was starting to spoon the dough onto the baking sheet when she frowned. Then her face cleared. She kept placing dough on the sheet.

"Oh." She blinked and met his eyes.

"What is it?" He stood up. "You hurt? Going to be sick? What?"

A look of wonder crossed her face. "I think I felt the baby move."

"What? Right now? Where?" He was at her side in an instant. He inspected her from head to toe, his gaze lingering on her stomach, but nothing looked different.

She turned to him. "Yes, I felt him."

He got lost in the green pools of her eyes. Everything he needed to know was in there. Relief. Amazement. And gratitude.

"How do you know?" His voice was low, gravelly.

She took his hand. Her soft touch nearly undid him. Then she placed it to the side of her belly.

"Just wait."

He held his breath, not because of the baby,

but because her warmth, her light touch, her floral perfume, all locked him in a trance.

And then he felt it. The tiniest flutter.

He jerked his hand back, his eyes opening wide.

He'd just felt her baby. A baby really was kicking in there!

He couldn't stop his mouth from curving into the biggest grin, and he tenderly placed his hand on her stomach again.

He waited.

And waited.

And there it was. The slightest of movements.

"Kit...your baby. He's there. Moving around." The awe of it overwhelmed him.

Her lips trembled, but joy streamed from her gaze. He wrapped her in his arms and held her close. She took a deep, wobbly breath, and relaxed her head against his shoulder. He held her for the longest time and it still wasn't long enough.

She leaned back, bringing her palms together in front of her lips, and shook her head as if she couldn't believe her good fortune.

"He's strong, Kitty Cat."

"I hope so."

"He is. Just like you."

Her eyes grew wide. "You think I'm strong?"

"I know you are."

She flung her arms around his neck and hugged him tightly. All he could think to do was keep her in his embrace. The proximity of her overloaded his senses, made him reflect on what he'd been thinking earlier— everyone had someone except him.

*She's your family.*

It was true, but this felt different. She'd been part of his family for many years, and he wasn't thinking of her as a sister. He certainly hoped she didn't think of him as a brother.

He was a man.

She was a woman.

And there was a baby between them.

Reality crushed his temples. The bills in the other room. The baby's heart problem.

For Sale signs and hospitals and a seedy apartment. Loving someone and never getting to say goodbye.

"I guess we'd better get these cookies in the oven." He stepped back and wiped his hand down his cheek.

Her lips curved into a wide smile. "I couldn't agree more."

Well, maybe it would be better for them both if she did view him as a brother. It would help him get over some of the emotional stuff her being here kicked up.

But…he still would prefer it if she'd see him as a man.

## Chapter Six

The following Friday, Kit enjoyed a grape Popsicle as she rocked on the front porch of her cabin. Wade had been gone most of the week. On Monday, he'd been busy on the ranch and then had an appointment in town with the real estate agent. He'd been tight-lipped about it when she'd asked that night. On Tuesday, he'd said he had business to catch up on and had holed up in his house most of the afternoon. Then on Wednesday, he'd left to move cattle for a few days. He was due back late tonight. While she missed his company, the days alone had given her precious time to get her bearings.

Now that she could feel the baby moving, her resolve to keep him alive and healthy had grown to borderline obsessive. Had she spent too much time searching the internet for pregnancy advice? Absolutely. She'd pored over forums of parents who'd had babies with the same diagnosis as hers until her eyes had glazed over. The testimonies simultaneously terrified her and filled her with hope.

What if the test results came back and her baby *did* have special needs? What if the hole in the heart was one of many health problems? What if— Oh, she had to stop this!

If only there was something she could do, a medicine to take, a diet that would cure his little heart…but her options were to be patient and wait, eat well, exercise, and get plenty of rest. Check. Check. And check.

All week she'd spent hours calling landlords about different apartments but hadn't found anyone willing to lease to her without her being employed. It looked as though she was stuck with the one she had. The thought depressed her more than she wanted to admit.

A drop of purple Popsicle fell onto her hand. She licked it off and finished the final bite. The sound of a vehicle rumbled closer.

A truck stopped at Wade's house. He'd had two deliveries this week already. The only other people who came around were Clint or Nash, to stop in and check on her. They'd brought supper for her while Wade had been gone. Lexi had come with Clint yesterday, and Kit had enjoyed her company. It still felt strange to have people go out of their way to help her, although she knew Wade had put them all up to it. She didn't mind. Being cared for was a nice change from life with Cam. And in a few short weeks, she'd be all alone again. Doing life on her own.

Her phone dinged. A text from Sandra came through. The package should arrive today. Enjoy!

The package—she'd forgotten about the baby items. She dialed Sandra's number.

"Hi, Kit, did you get the box?" Sandra sounded out of breath.

"Something was dropped off to the main house of the ranch where I'm staying. I'll head over in a few minutes. I just wanted to thank you for going to all the trouble to get it here."

"It was no trouble. I hope you enjoy all the goodies."

The goodies. She wouldn't think about them yet. "How is your summer going?"

"Busy. Now that Greta graduated, it's all I can do to keep on top of her college plans. Orientation is next week already. How did that happen? When your baby is born, try not to blink. It goes so quickly. Anyway, how are you feeling? I miss you. It was always nice seeing your smiling face at the school."

"I miss you, too." And, surprisingly, she did. She hadn't made much effort with the teachers, but since she'd been away for a few weeks, she missed the interaction with them, however small it had been. "What is Greta studying?"

"She has no clue. She talks about getting a business degree, then claims she's going to be a doctor. Honestly, I don't care at this point. Just pick something, you know? It's a shame she didn't get the teaching bug."

Kit chuckled. "I had that particular bug since I was a little girl."

"Me, too, Kit. For as long as I can remember." A voice shouted in the background. "Frank's calling. I've got to go. Sorry to cut this short. You take care now, you hear?"

"You, too, and congratulations about Greta graduating."

They hung up, and she rested the phone on the arm of the rocking chair. Sandra's package was probably sitting on Wade's front porch right now. She might as well go up there and see for herself.

Pushing herself to a standing position, she assessed her body. Everything seemed fine. The baby hadn't kicked in hours, but his kicks were sporadic at best. Her flip-flops probably weren't the best option to walk up the gravel drive; she'd better change.

She slipped into her favorite cowboy boots and meandered up the drive to Wade's house. New wildflowers had popped up—crimson flames of Indian paintbrush, delicate periwinkle of blue flax and splashes of yellow from balsamroot. A hawk circled overhead.

Peace.

This place radiated peace.

How she'd longed for peace her entire life.

It wouldn't last. Never did. But she wished she could scoop up this feeling and put it in a jar to sprinkle out whenever the hard times hit.

She skirted Wade's garage and climbed the two steps to the porch. A large box stood near the door. Bending slightly and pushing her hair over her shoulder, she read the label. It was addressed to Kit McAllistor.

Now what?

She hadn't expected such a large package. She couldn't carry it to her cabin. And she didn't feel like walking back to get her car.

Wade wouldn't care if she opened the box in his house and came back for it later.

Back at the garage, she typed in the key code and strode to the door leading to the kitchen. Then she continued through the living room and hallway to the front entrance. After dragging the package inside, she pushed it to the living room near one of the couches.

She remembered seeing scissors in a kitchen drawer. A few moments later, she was on her knees near the box with the scissors poised to cut through the packing tape. But she held back.

Was she ready for this?

Her hopes had already been soaring since the very first fluttery kick. Was it wise to open this box of delights and sink into the delicious sensation of actually being able to use the contents?

Maybe she should wait until the microarray test results came back. Then she wouldn't get wrapped into dreams, only to be crushed by them later.

She set the scissors on the package and slowly made her way back to the garage. She shut the door and plodded back to her cabin. The sun didn't seem as bright as it had earlier.

At some point in her life, she'd look forward to something without worrying about it being snatched from her. Until then, protecting herself from the pain was the best way forward. Which meant it was high time she sealed up her heart. Wade's sweet reaction at feeling the baby kick had allowed longing to shimmy in where the shards of her broken dreams with Cam still lay.

She'd be leaving this ranch in a few weeks. Wade would be here. And she'd be going through life on her own. Again.

Yawning, Wade headed out to the kitchen as the sun rose Saturday morning. The past three days had been exhilarating and exhausting. Moving cattle to their summer pasture made him feel alive. Riding with the other cowboys, taking a good look at the entire outfit, watching for cows acting out of the ordinary and making sure they were all healthy, gave him a purpose. Reminded him his dream had always revolved around ranching in Wyoming. It had also given him clarity about the bills he'd finally tallied.

JPX Ranch was on the market, but, for now, it wasn't being advertised. He'd told Ray not to put the sign up, and if anyone wanted to come tour the property, Wade would make sure Kit wasn't around.

All week his mind kept tripping back to her. Wondering how she was doing. Marveling at feeling her baby kick. Chastising himself for caring so much.

At least his friends had checked on her while he was gone. He'd actually grown panicky at the thought of her getting cramps or falling and being in pain for days without anyone around to help. Asking Clint and Nash to check on her had been the only way he'd been able to keep his anxiety under control.

He poured water into the coffee maker,

dumped scoops of grounds into the filter and flipped on the switch. Light began streaming in through the windows, and his gaze fell on a big box next to the couch. He hadn't noticed it last night when he'd arrived. He'd driven in around two in the morning, and he'd been so bleary-eyed it was a wonder he'd found his bed.

With a yawn, he inspected the package. Addressed to Kit. Must be the baby things she'd mentioned. Weird she hadn't opened it.

He rubbed his chin. Had she gotten bad news and hadn't told him? Doubtful. Then why would she have gone to the trouble of lugging it in here and getting the scissors? She must be scared. He really didn't blame her.

He was scared, too. And it wasn't even his baby.

Maybe she needed a distraction from her troubles. He'd take her…where? Town didn't excite him. Too many people. From the looks of it outside, the weather would be fine. What about a picnic at the river later?

She'd always liked being outdoors. Wade returned to the kitchen and poured a large mug of coffee. He took it out to the front porch and sat on one of the chairs. The land splayed before him in ridges and valleys. The riot of meadow colors would be gone soon, leaving behind dry grass, sage and patches of red earth.

Would he have to say goodbye to all this? Even considering the prospect made Wade's palms clammy. He'd spent a small fortune renovating the house and all the outbuildings. This was his home. His life was here.

If someone bought JPX Ranch, he would have to move. Dudley Farms would mean a huge life change. He didn't want to say goodbye to cattle ranching. And he hated the thought of being hours away from his friends.

Sorrow made him bow his head. *God, I don't want to lose this ranch. I don't think I've ever appreciated it the way I do right this minute.*

For a moment, his entire being filled with

gratitude, which didn't make sense. Why would he be grateful when he likely would have to sell it?

*God, what's going on? Am I cracking up?*

Dottie's voice from back in his Yearling days ran through his mind. He'd been going through a tough time the year after he and Kit were separated, and Dottie had slid a plate of cookies his way. *God created everything, champ. I figure He's got your life under control. We can praise Him through sunshine and storms.*

Sunshine and storms. Most of his adult life had been sunshine. His childhood had been storms. Both had brought him where he was today. Without overthinking it, he simply bowed his head and thanked the Lord. For these quiet moments. For today.

He sipped the rich coffee and let his mind wander. He'd been introduced to church and God by Dottie and Big Bob. He remembered the warmth in his heart as he read the Bible with her. He'd gotten baptized. For a long time, he'd made prayer a priority in his life. When had he stopped?

Probably when he stopped going to church.

Avoiding church hadn't been a conscious decision. Life had called. Ambition had driven out any leisure hours as he'd scrimped and saved to buy his first tiny ranch, where the shack still stood. Success upon success had allowed him to expand, and Jackson's ranch had driven him to financial gain he'd never thought possible at his age.

Had he ever thanked God for any of it?

The coffee tasted like vinegar as it slid down his throat.

*I know it's late, but I'm truly grateful for all You've blessed me with, Lord. Don't take it away from me.*

He stayed on the porch a long time, letting the uncertainties and anxieties dissipate. Finally, he checked the time. Almost eight thirty. Maybe Ray would have an update for him.

He went inside, found his cell phone and returned to the front porch. Pressed Ray's number and waited. Two rings. He took a drink. Three rings. Man, he needed a shower. Four rings.

"Ray Simon speaking." His crisp voice was all business.

"What's the scoop on the couple looking for a ranch?" Wade asked. "Good news, I hope."

"Sorry, no news here. I've talked to their real estate agent. They plan on touring both your properties. They haven't been out to see Dudley Farms yet."

"Yet, huh? That means there's still hope."

"I wouldn't count on them wanting Dudley Farms. They're young and ambitious. Looking for land with multiple guest cottages on it. In addition to ranching, they want to host high-end corporate bonding retreats."

He let the news sink in. "Obviously, my ranch is better suited for that. Dudley Farms only has the house and outbuildings. Nothing livable besides the main house."

"Right," Ray said. "And the location isn't

ideal, either. They have family over in Cody. They'd like to be closer to them."

"Sweet Dreams would be an easy drive." A pit grew in his stomach. "Do they have the money to purchase either of my properties?"

"Yeah. They're newlyweds. It's my understanding he inherited a lot of money from his late grandfather."

"Does he even know how to ranch?" The thought of nonranchers coming in and ruining this operation made him sick.

"I'm not sure about him. He owns a corporate retreat business. He's very successful at it. The wife grew up on a cattle ranch in Oklahoma."

Well, at least one of them would know what they were doing.

"Are there any other potential buyers for Dudley Farms?" He knew the answer, but had to ask anyway.

"A big game hunter is still looking at properties. Another couple has been eyeing land near Montana. Other than that, no new buyers that I've heard of."

"Okay."

"I'm doing everything I can, Wade. I created new flyers to appeal to the corporate retreat angle of JPX Ranch."

"You know the minimum amount I need."

"I know." Papers rustled in the background. "Would you still want to sell Dudley Farms if JPX sells?"

He really didn't want to start over there. His life was here.

Why had he ever bought that property? If he could go back and do it all over…

"I'm not sure."

"Think about it and let me know."

"Thanks, Ray."

He could always move back to the shack and the hundred acres that started it all. Then his failure would be complete.

He needed a distraction as much as Kit did. He'd drag her out for a picnic if she even hinted at saying no.

"Thank you for suggesting this." Kit tucked a rolled quilt under her arm, while

Wade carried a cooler in one hand and a large tote bag in the other. They walked through green grass toward the river—more a stream—on the east end of Wade's ranch. A wooden bridge arched over the river, and trees full of green leaves crowded the banks. Cottonwoods, aspen and lodgepole pines provided cover for the singing birds flitting about.

"I figured you could use a change in scenery." A heather-gray T-shirt stretched across his chest. "This is one of my favorite spots."

"You come here often?"

"Not as often as I'd like."

"Busy, busy." She kept her pace slow. She wasn't in a hurry and hadn't been in a few weeks, which was a huge contrast from when she'd been working.

Every day had been like running a marathon. As soon as the alarm went off, she'd jump out of bed, get ready, pack a lunch, slurp down coffee on the drive to the school, prep her lessons, try to engage the children, grade papers, take calls, make lesson plans, come home and crash. Evenings were spent making dinner, eating it in silence—sometimes alone, sometimes with Cam—telling herself she should exercise but not actually finding the energy to do so, and either binge-watching television shows or surfing the internet until falling into bed, to do it all over again the next day.

How had she managed to live for years in such an unfulfilling routine?

The routine had been comfortable. She'd known what to expect. This new life was unpredictable, scary and forcing her to rely on God in ways she hadn't since she was a child.

"What do you think? Is this a good spot?" Wade pointed to a flat stretch of lawn on the bank. The view of the river was unobstructed. Gurgling water added to the peaceful scene.

"Perfect." She unrolled the quilt, and he took an end from her hands. Together, they spread it on the ground.

"Take a seat. I'll dish out the food."

She lowered herself to the quilt before easing back to a seated position. He poked around in the cooler and tote bag. A few minutes later, he handed her a plate.

After thanking him, she took a bite of a sandwich. Delicious. The air was hot, but a gentle breeze from the river kept it from being oppressive.

"This reminds me of the picnics we'd take down at the Bradleys' creek." She kicked off her sandals and wiggled her toes on the quilt.

He finished chewing a potato chip. "We'd sneak soda crackers and those cheese slices wrapped in plastic."

"I'd hardly call that cheese."

"Back then you did." He grinned. "You'd break the slices into quarters and layer them between the crackers. What did you call them?"

"Finger sandwiches. I'd read about fancy luncheons in a book. I thought they were high society."

"They were." He popped a red grape in his mouth.

She thought back to the one picnic that had seared itself into her mind. It was the day they'd swapped their growing-up stories. Neither of them had liked to talk about their past, and they'd decided to come clean with each other on the promise they would never discuss them again.

"Remember the day we told each other our stories?" she asked.

"Yeah." He grew pensive.

"Does the promise still hold?" She could practically see him all those years ago, handsome in a baby-faced way, and, boy, had he been scrappy. He'd sat next to her on a torn blanket. They'd both had their knees tucked up and their arms around their legs. Neither had looked at the other while they spoke.

This scene felt the same as all those years ago.

"A promise is a promise," he said quietly.

Fair enough. She'd memorized his tale, anyhow. He'd been born to a teenage unwed mother who'd waited tables at a truck stop to support them. He'd been four years old when she vanished. Police had speculated she'd run off with someone. Shortly after, he was placed in a foster home. A year later, her remains were found in Utah. She hadn't run off; she'd been kidnapped and murdered. Wade had lived in two other homes before ending up at the Bradleys' with Kit.

"Well, I kept one story to myself that day." She sat up, trying to tuck her knees to her chest, but the baby was in the way. She kept her legs straight out before her instead.

"Good story or bad story?" He turned to her, his eyes full of compassion.

She'd always told him the good stories, embellishing if necessary. Making him happy had made her happy back then. She still wanted to bring him joy, but the truth was more important now.

"Bad."

He bent his knees and wrapped his arms around them, sitting next to her, the same as he had long ago. "Go ahead. You can tell me."

"Remember how I told you about Aunt Martha?"

"Yeah." He flicked a glance her way.

"I lied about her."

"Which part?"

"The her-being-nice part. She beat me, screamed at me. Told me she'd whip the bad out of me. Every single day."

He blinked, his jaw shifting.

"Deep down, I believed she was right. Why else would my birth mom leave me there as a baby? I thought I deserved the belt."

"The belt?" He stared ahead, his jaw clenching. "How long? How long were you there?" His voice was low, gruff.

"Until I was five, almost six. My teacher saw the bruises. The belt marks. I was removed from her home shortly after."

"I liked your original story better."

"The one where she died peacefully in her

sleep after loving me like I was her own little girl?" Kit attempted a smile.

"Yeah." He put his arm over her shoulders and gave her a sideways hug. "I'm sorry. Physical and emotional abuse is never okay."

"I agree. Looking back, I think she may have had mental issues. She'd be nice one minute and a terror the next. I lived in a constant state of fear and didn't even know it. I came to expect hot and cold behavior from everyone around me."

"You shouldn't have gone through that. You didn't deserve it. No one does."

Her throat tightened. Hearing him say those words was like a healing balm on a long-festering wound.

"It affected me. I never felt wanted. I thought there was something wrong with me." Why had she said that out loud?

He nodded, swallowing. "I didn't, either."

"You didn't?" She couldn't imagine this confident, successful man ever feeling unworthy.

"I may have left out a story from my past,

too." He shifted to face her. His blue eyes shone bright with intensity. "My second foster home was abusive."

She reached over and squeezed his hand. He held it tightly. She wanted to take the pain from him, to go back in time and give whoever did that to him a piece of her mind. "I'm sorry. I hate that you went through it."

"I hate the same for you," he said. "The day I met you was the best day of my life. You're going to get it right. You know, with your baby. He won't know the cruelty we faced."

Meeting her was the best day of his life? The words filled a hole in her soul she hadn't known was there. Meeting him had taken her life from lonely and gray to bright and exciting. Wade had always been the best thing that had ever happened to her.

She rubbed her belly. "I'll do everything I can to protect him, but if he has special needs, he could face a different type of cruelty."

Wade sighed, letting go of her hand. "I

know. I don't like it. I guess you could home-school if things got bad. You're the teacher, right?"

"I'm trying not to put too much thought into the future until I have more information."

"Information is good." He leaned back on his elbows, extending his legs out. "I've been thinking about that property I mentioned a while back, Dudley Farms."

"Oh, yeah?"

"If Ray doesn't find a buyer for it, I might move."

"I thought your dreams were wrapped up here. Don't you like ranching anymore?"

"I love ranching. It's in my blood."

"Then what would happen to this ranch? It's yours. It was meant to be yours."

Pain flashed across his face so quickly she thought she imagined it. Had she said something to upset him?

"Maybe I need something new. I could try farming." His teasing tone didn't fool her.

Something wasn't right, but if he didn't want to tell her, she wouldn't drag it out of him.

"Should I start calling you Farmer Croft?"

"Yep." He chuckled. "By the way, why didn't you open the package in the middle of my living room? Did you expect me to do the honors or something?"

Her face grew warm. "No, I… Well, this sounds pathetic, but I chickened out."

"Diapers scare you that much?"

"Very funny." She swatted his arm. "No, it's my warped way of thinking. If I get my hopes up, they'll come crashing down. I don't know if I can handle any more bad news at this point in my life."

He lay back, his head resting in his palms, elbows wide. "You'll be fine. Just open it. I'll help you. A few baby bottles won't give you a breakdown."

She drew her eyebrows together and mindlessly plucked a stem of wild blue flax. Maybe he was right. Was she over-thinking the baby supplies? A part of her shouted, *"No, don't do it!"* But the logical side scolded her for being a ninny.

Trying to anticipate her reaction to opening the package was giving her a headache. Her original plan of opening the box *after* finding out the results of the tests seemed the best choice. They would be in soon. Sure, she feared the worst, but shouldn't she at least be preparing for the baby's arrival? Why was she dragging her feet?

*Because I can't bear to have this baby ripped from me.*

A butterfly caught her attention as it flitted to a flower, then flew haphazardly away. This picnic spot was an oasis. No more worrying about the baby.

She glanced over at Wade. His eyes were closed, and his chest expanded and relaxed in regular intervals. He looked at peace. Still a big hunk of muscular man. But beneath it all, she could see the young boy she'd bonded with.

Who took care of him out on this secluded ranch? Was he lonely? Was that why he was talking about selling it? And what was this talk about farming?

She couldn't picture him on anything but a horse.

Who did he have to comfort him on the bad days?

Did he even have bad days?

She sighed. Everyone had bad days. She and Wade had just gotten used to hiding them. They'd gotten used to hiding a lot of things because of their childhoods.

Did he suppress his emotions the way she did? Keep the most important stuff to himself?

She wanted to know his most important stuff. She'd wanted to know it from the minute she'd met him.

But she wasn't an optimistic little girl anymore. She came with issues. Problems. And she wouldn't burden him with those, too.

She kissed the tips of two of her fingers and placed them on his forehead. *Rest up. You earned it.*

## Chapter Seven

He was going to get her to open the box even if it meant bribing and cajoling. The woman needed to face reality—she was having a baby. And that meant she had to start preparing for it. No more of this protecting-herself-from-the-pain-of-possibly-losing-the-child nonsense. Did she really think avoiding the box would somehow prevent her from being devastated if the baby didn't make it?

Wade washed his hands in the kitchen sink. Supper was almost ready. He'd set the table earlier. He'd drive to the cabin to get her in a minute.

This morning at church, he'd actually listened to half the sermon before his mind started wandering. He hadn't liked where it had traveled. Right up there to the front of the church where his buddies had gotten married. The look of love on their brides' faces when they'd said their vows had etched into his memory.

All the tuxedos he'd had to rent recently must have rubbed romance dust off on him or something. Couldn't have happened at a worse time, either. His life was collapsing around him.

What did he have to offer a woman?

*A* woman? Like there was anyone besides Kit he'd even consider spending his days with. But after all she'd been through in life, she deserved someone who would protect her from problems, not someone who would add to them.

They'd skipped the group breakfast at the diner when Kit complained of feeling a bit low. What did "a bit low" mean? He had no clue, but he'd sure spent enough time trying to figure it out today. Worrying hadn't been his style until recently. He'd finally gotten sick of himself and had prayed for a clear head. He was tired of feeling strung out. Tired enough to ask God for help.

Two knocks on the glass of the patio door and a sliding sound drew his attention to the dining area.

"It smells so good in here." Kit's cheeks were pink, but worry clouded her eyes. "Whatcha cookin'?"

"A slab of beef. Brisket, to be precise. Been in there for hours. Why didn't you wait for me to pick you up?"

"Yum. What can I do?"

It didn't escape his notice that she ignored his question. It was on the tip of his tongue to say, *"First of all, you can stay off your feet and let me drive you, and second, you can open that big box in my living room,"* but he didn't. "Grab a seat. I'll bring the food over."

He carried a platter of sliced brisket with

potatoes and carrots to the table. After Kit said grace, they both dug in.

"What did you do this afternoon?" she asked.

"Rode Thunder."

"It's been forever and a day since I rode a horse."

He scooped a bite of potato on his fork. "You miss it?"

"Yeah. I always enjoyed riding. It seemed like all my friends had their own horses."

"Any time you get an itch to ride, let me know." He frowned, growing tense. "After you have the baby, of course. Don't want anything happening to you or the little guy."

"Don't worry." She smiled, shaking salt on the vegetables. "I have no desire to ride one now."

The tension in his neck eased.

"Maybe after the baby is born I can come visit." The words sounded choked. "I'll be moving in a few weeks."

It didn't seem like nearly enough time with her.

"You found a different apartment?" He dug into the brisket.

"I'm meeting with the heart specialist in a few weeks. I'll need to be in Casper by then."

"You didn't answer my question." He knew he sounded testy, but he hadn't realized she still planned to move to that nasty apartment. A roach-infested hovel if he ever saw one.

"I meet with the cardiologist three weeks from Tuesday, and I have an appointment with an obstetrician the following Thursday."

He lunged for the glass of water. Three weeks? They'd fly by faster than a hawk with a field mouse. Man, he was jumpy.

"Let me know when you want to check out apartments. I'll drive you there."

"Wade, I'm moving in to the one I put the deposit on."

"No way." He leaned in. "I want you and the baby safe."

"We'll be safe. God always watches over

me." The gleam in her eye as she nodded just about did him in. She looked like she was trying to convince herself as much as she was trying to convince him.

"It's not the place for you—"

"It is." Her quiet words were harder than steel. "I told you, I don't have a lot of options. I have no job and I need to be near the hospital."

"I'll cover the deposit for a better apartment and the difference in rent. You can't live there." And she couldn't. He knew it down to the bottom of his toes.

He *had* to sell one of his properties soon. It wasn't too much to ask, was it? He still had a few weeks before Kit moved. And selling Del Poncho would free up some cash.

She blinked several times. "It's kind of you, Wade, but I can't accept it."

"You can't accept it?" His chest hollowed out. Was he some stranger she couldn't trust? Didn't friends help each other? "Oh, that's right. You don't accept help from anyone, including me."

"I'm here, aren't I?" Her eyes flashed.

"As a last resort." He leaned back and cocked his head toward the living room. "What about the package over there? Someone took the time to buy those gifts and send them here, but opening it would be accepting help, wouldn't it? And we both know you don't take charity."

"That's not it—"

"Prove it, then. Open the box."

"I don't think this is the right time. I'll take it back to my cabin and—"

"Kit."

She hated when he used that tone. He was wrong. She could accept help. She could.

Then why was it so hard to open this package?

Presents she'd unwrapped over the years rushed back. Gifts that had been stolen by other kids or lost when she'd been forced to move. If she opened this package, would her dream of becoming a mother be stolen, too? Would she get her hopes up, only to lose the baby?

*It's just a box. You're giving it too much power. It's cardboard, Kit. Come on.*

"Fine. I'll do it now." She marched to the kitchen, snatched the scissors out of the drawer and headed to the living room.

She knelt next to the box. Carefully cut through the packing tape. When the flaps were free, she sat back on her heels for a moment. She was going to love every item in here, and if the baby died, each gift would hurt that much more.

*God, I'm scared. Please help me see this for what it is, not for what I think it represents.*

"What are you waiting for?"

"Nothing." She lifted one flap. Then the other. And, taking a deep breath, peered into the box.

A crocheted white baby blanket covered the top. She tenderly lifted it and brought it to her chin. It was so soft. Beautiful. Tears pricked her eyes. Someone had made this for her child. The hours it must have taken. The generosity.

Wade let out a low whistle. "Someone was feeling confident. White? With a baby? I don't think it will stay clean for long."

She let out a shaky laugh, not trusting herself to reply.

"Is that it?" He made a production of craning his neck to peek inside. "Seems like an awfully big box for one blanket."

She gave him a fake glare. "Don't rush me." She could do this. Now that the first item was out, she could handle the rest.

She reached in again and pulled out a package of bottles. One by one, she brought out the treasures. Newborn-sized diapers, a pack of onesies, rattles, bibs, a mobile, a sleeper with yellow duckies, a floppy stuffed dog, pacifiers and, at the bottom, a card in a purple envelope. She'd wait to read it at the cabin. If she opened it now and saw all the signatures of the people she'd worked with for years and hadn't truly appreciated, she'd lose it.

Wade was right. She'd never been able to accept help. What had she lost out on over the years because of it?

"What do you do with this?" Wade held the box with the mobile. His grimace was priceless.

"It attaches to the baby's crib. The little fish dangle from it as it turns. I think it makes music, too."

He squinted at the back of the box. "Yep. It needs two AA batteries."

Carefully, she placed everything back inside, then pressed the blanket to her chest once more.

"If the baby doesn't make it, I'm keeping this no matter what." She rubbed the soft material against her cheek. "Then I won't forget."

"You won't forget. You'd never forget."

She lowered her lashes, nodding. He was right, of course.

"But you should keep it. It's real nice." He cleared his throat. "And don't even think along those lines. He'll make it."

She wasn't sure. Women had stillborn babies on a regular basis, and her baby already had been diagnosed with problems. The idea of losing her son and having to give birth to his lifeless body had kept her up many nights.

"I'm becoming grim and pessimistic, Wade," she said quietly. "I try not to think of all the things that could go wrong, but there they are. In my head, waiting to pounce. And then I can't stop thinking about them. And I try to get answers on the internet, and…"

"Well, there's your problem. Don't go on the internet. You'll only find a million more reasons to be scared. I had a pain in my abdomen, and I went on one of those doctor websites, thinking it might be my appendix. Two hours later, I was convinced I had either intestinal worms or cancer. Worst night I've had in a while. Stay off the internet."

"I know you're right, but…"

"Can't you just enjoy this? I mean, a baby is growing inside you. Doesn't it count for something? If the worst happens, you *will* be devastated. Period. You can't prevent the pain by worrying about it beforehand."

She hadn't thought of it in those terms. "So you're saying whether I enjoy the pregnancy or worry my way through it, the outcome will be the same? And I should be thankful for each moment?"

"Yeah."

"What if you're wrong?"

"I'm never wrong. You know that." His white teeth gleamed through his smile.

She'd let that one slide. "I hate feeling so…helpless. There's nothing I can do to fix this."

"Well, there is one thing." He grew serious. "I mean, besides eating healthy and getting rest."

"What?"

"I know you have a strong faith. I know you pray. When I was at Yearling, Dottie told me over and over that God hears our prayers."

"But I don't always like His answer."

"This morning the preacher said you can take everything to God in prayer."

"Do you?" She watched him carefully. He'd never been overtly religious. He'd even admitted to her he hadn't regularly attended church in years. But it didn't mean he lacked faith.

"No, I don't." He looked toward the windows.

"Why not?" Her knees started burning, so she lugged herself up and sat on the couch, keeping the crocheted baby blanket folded on her lap.

"I don't know." He rubbed his chin. "I guess I rely on myself."

It made sense in a way. Wade had everything he'd ever wanted. A big house, huge ranch, oodles of property, freedom, friends—maybe he didn't feel the need to pray.

"What about when something is out of your power to handle or fix?"

He shrugged. "Doesn't happen very often."

Hmm...was he missing the point? He

wasn't in control of his life. No one was. "Well, God isn't just here for our problems. I used to only rely on Him in times of trouble, but I realized I was missing out."

He frowned. "Missing out on what?"

"When things started going south with Cam, I relied on God more and more. I started seeing His everyday mercies. Eventually, I realized I finally had the dad I'd always wanted."

"Dad, huh?" The confusion on Wade's face lingered.

"Yeah, He's my loving Father."

"If you're convinced He's so loving, why are you worried?"

The question made her pause. "Life doesn't always turn out the way we want."

"Sometimes it does, though."

"I know." He didn't get it. The rules were different for her than they were for other people. Her dreams had been crushed on a regular basis for as long as she could remember. And after the way she yelled at Cam?

Well, there were consequences for her sins. "I don't deserve it."

"That's silly. You do deserve it."

"What if I'm being punished?"

"For what?"

"The things I screamed at Cam." She choked on the last words. Why was it so hard to admit her mistakes?

"You're not being punished. Don't you believe in forgiveness?"

"Of course I believe in forgiveness. Jesus died on the cross and rose again for my sins. I'm forgiven."

"Then why are you holding on to this guilt?"

"Because a sin is a sin. And I'm not holding on to guilt." The last line didn't come out very strong. Was that what she was doing? "I'm not. Let's drop it."

He stared at her thoughtfully a moment, then gestured to the box. "What else do you need for the baby?"

"I'm not sure. I'll think about it another time." She placed the blanket back on top of the items and closed the flaps. "Can we just sit on your patio and watch the countryside?"

"If that's what you want."

She did. She was tired of thinking and talking. Tired of it all.

# Chapter Eight

Babies sure needed an awful lot of stuff.

Wade tucked the list of supplies he'd jot-
ted last night into his pocket as he strode
down the lane toward Kit's cabin Monday
afternoon. She might not be fired up about
shopping for the tyke, but Wade didn't want
her waiting until the last minute and bringing the baby home to nothing. If he could
convince her to go shopping with him, he'd
sleep easier.

And sleep had been a tricky minx last
night. Why he couldn't get Kit's words
about praying and seeing the everyday mercies out of his mind, he couldn't say. One

thing he did know? He'd taken his blessings for granted. All night his conscience had weighed heavily. Finally, he'd gotten up, stared out the window at the full moon and thanked God for his health and friends. He'd also prayed for Dudley Farms to sell so he wouldn't have to give up the ranch. He wished he could say he felt peace—that God would surely provide the buyer he'd asked for—but he didn't.

A morning of ranch work had given him a reprieve from his thoughts. At this point, he needed the distraction of baby shopping more than Kit did.

He closed the distance to her cabin. Usually at this time in the afternoon she'd be rocking on her porch. But she wasn't out there. He didn't want to wake her if she was napping. Wanted her to get as much rest as possible. He loped up the porch steps and knocked quietly on her door.

A few moments later, she opened it, beckoning him to come inside. She held her cell phone to her ear. He entered, closing the door behind him as quietly as possible. Then he took a seat on her couch, trying not to eavesdrop on her conversation and failing miserably.

"And what does that mean?" Her voice sounded strained. "Uh-huh. Okay. And you're sure about the numbers?"

She hurried to the dining table and wrote something on a sticky pad. He narrowed his eyes. What was going on? Her hair was pulled back in a messy bun, and she wore khaki shorts with a billowy bubblegum-pink shirt.

"Do I need to send everything over?" She straightened, biting her lower lip. "You will? Thank you. And thanks for calling."

A few seconds later, she ended the call and whirled to face him. She opened her arms wide, her face shining. "The baby doesn't have special needs!"

No special needs! The implications hit him one by one like a lighted pathway up to his heart.

He hustled over to her and hauled her into

his arms. Lifting her, he twirled her off her toes as she laughed and wrapped her arms around his neck. Then he set her down. Her eyes darkened, and the hope within them exploded to life the emotions he'd dammed. She radiated relief and joy and all the things he wanted her to have. Without thinking, he got down on his knees.

Gently, he placed his hands on the sides of her belly and planted a kiss in the middle.

"Junior, you keep growing, you hear me? You're going to be strong. This hole you've got in your heart won't slow you down. You're made with your mama's steel, and trust me, she's something."

Still on his knees, he lifted his gaze. Kit's smile was full of tenderness as she lightly brushed her fingers over his hair. Compassion, understanding and happiness—all for him. He could feel it as sure as he could feel the hardwood floor beneath his knees.

He stood up and hugged her again.

"I'm starting to believe the baby might actually be okay." The words were tentative, as if she feared saying them aloud would bring down thunder and lightning.

"Does this mean the hole has a better chance of healing on its own?"

"No, I wish it did. But at least I don't have to worry about Down syndrome or, worse, DiGeorge syndrome."

"Whatever happens, I'm here for you."

Her face flushed as she gave him a quick smile.

"Let's sit and you can tell me everything." Taking a seat on the couch, he rested his elbows on his knees while she sat in the chair kitty-corner to him.

"There's not much to tell. The chromosomal microarray test didn't indicate any genetic mutations. I'm so relieved. The hole in the heart might simply be an abnormality." She averted her eyes. "Sorry, all of this gets me choked up."

"Hey, no need to apologize. I know how worried you've been. I worry, too. This is big news. Good news."

"It is." She beamed, nodding.

He remembered the list in his pocket. What better time to bring up shopping than now, while she was optimistic?

"I hope you're ready to get serious about having this baby." He pretended to be stern.

"Get serious?" She huffed. "I couldn't be any more serious."

"Well, then you're going to have to prove it." He unfolded the paper and snapped it open, holding it out to her. "I did a little investigating, and the box of baby things? Not even close to what you need. It's time to go shopping."

Her mouth dropped open. "You came up with a list of baby items I need?"

"I did." He nodded firmly.

"You're telling me you went online and searched for what parents should have on hand for newborns."

"Yes. Why is that so hard for you to grasp?"

Her eyebrows soared to her forehead. "It's just…you're a bachelor. I don't remember the last time you mentioned a girlfriend, and I didn't picture you being interested in domestic stuff. How many times did you say you didn't see yourself married?"

Domestic stuff. For years, he'd shut out all thoughts of domesticity, focusing instead on expanding his ranching empire.

But tucked beneath all those layers, a part of him cried out to have what his friends had—love, marriage, a partner, babies.

His mother had barely been out of her teens when she'd been kidnapped and murdered. If she'd had someone looking out for her—someone financially supporting her—she wouldn't have had to work in a dive restaurant at the truck stop or live in a sketchy apartment on the wrong side of town.

Kit's apartment in Casper was no better. No safer.

"I might not be Mr. Domestic, but it doesn't mean I can't help you out."

"If you wanted to be Mr. Domestic, you could be. You'd make a great daddy."

Him? *Make a great daddy?* He needed to

beat down the desire those words were puffing up before he started believing them.

His cell phone rang. He whipped it out of his pocket and checked the caller. Ray. Maybe it was a day for good news. Mr. Domestic wouldn't be possible until Mr. Overextended's circumstances changed. And even then he doubted he could embrace the vulnerability inherent in loving a woman.

"Hello?" Lifting one finger to indicate he'd be back in a minute, he went out onto the porch, where he could talk in private.

"The young couple I mentioned wants to see both your ranch and Dudley Farms."

Music to his ears. And yet his stomach dropped. It meant possibly saying goodbye to the life he'd built.

"Be prepared for an offer," Ray said. "I'd be shocked if they don't jump at the chance to own JPX Ranch. It checks off almost everything on their list."

"Thanks, Ray." He stared out at the mountains, took in the land, his house in the distance, the other cabins down the way. Why hadn't he thought it was enough? "Go ahead and set up the appointments."

"I will. Hopefully, you'll have a solid contract on one of them soon."

"Yeah, and I'm hoping it's on the other one."

"If they do make you an offer on your ranch, are you mentally prepared to accept it?"

Was he? Jackson's face and raspy voice as they'd ridden around the property all those months before Jackson died rushed back. They'd bonded. Two bachelors—one old, one young—both with a deep connection to this patch of Wyoming. Jackson would be appalled at the thought of his life's work being handed over to strangers.

The bills Wade had tallied, the seriousness of his cash flow problem, came to mind.

"I'm prepared." The words sank like a boulder in his gut. He had to sell—one or the other—soon, or he'd lose it all.

"Good. If you have any questions, call

me. I'll let you know when they want to come out."

"Thanks, Ray."

"No problem."

He hung up, tucking the phone back in his pocket.

The day was as bright as could be, but he could feel a charge in the air. Stifling heat. A storm might be brewing.

He'd better take Kit to buy those baby supplies. He might be a bachelor without any plans for a wife and kids, but he was also a friend, and he'd be a real heel if he let Kit down.

Kit and the baby meant more to him than…

He gulped. They might mean the world to him, but who was he kidding? He couldn't be more than Uncle Wade.

Was it enough?

Maybe he'd better make time to pray. Not just about selling the ranch, but about Kit and her baby, too. He had a lot to think about.

* * *

The man had done it again. Taken a phone call in the middle of their conversation and left her high and dry, as if whoever was calling was the president of the United States.

Did she have a Don't Mind Me, I'm Invisible sign on her forehead?

And here she'd been all gushy and full of joy because her baby was okay! And Wade had dropped to his knees to kiss her belly and talk to her unborn son. The gesture had been so completely unexpected, so sweet and endearing, she'd almost tugged him back to a standing position to kiss him senseless.

She could *not* kiss Wade.

Even if he was the polar opposite of Cam.

Cam, who'd shown few signs of physical affection. Cam, who'd forgotten their wedding anniversary two years in a row. Cam, who'd looked her in the eye when she'd presented him with the pregnancy test and flatly told her he didn't want the baby and didn't want to share custody, either.

*He's dead. Can you really not remember any good things about him?*

It was easier remembering the bad. Hanging on to her hurts. But was it good for her?

She reached way back in her memories to when they'd met. He'd had an air about him—a confidence she'd liked. And he'd looked at her like she was something special. Their initial dates had been fun, but then, Cam had been fun…at first. They'd done things—snowboarded, went bowling, played intramural volleyball on Tuesday nights at the university. She'd enjoyed hearing about his family—his father and brother. And they'd fallen into an easy relationship. He wasn't clingy, and neither was she.

But his lack of clinginess had only been a sign she hadn't recognized. He hadn't been stuck to her like glue because he hadn't really needed her.

For the umpteenth time she wondered why he'd married her. Why?

She'd probably never know.

Her gaze fell on the paper Wade had left

on the coffee table. She smoothed it out and, as she read it, her annoyance at him for taking the call vanished.

In his chicken-scratch handwriting, he'd listed a full page of things the baby needed. Diaper cream. A crib. Wipes. Burp cloths. Thermometer. Changing table. On and on it went.

Why did Wade have to be so kind? And gorgeous? And thoughtful?

And off-limits.

She gripped the paper in her hands.

She couldn't fall for him. She'd be in another unfulfilling relationship. He felt sorry for her because of the baby, and he cared for her because he always had—but love? He didn't love her, not the way she needed.

Her relationship with Cam had been bad. If she messed things up by getting romantic with Wade, she'd lose her best friend.

She couldn't handle losing him, too.

She glanced down at her belly, growing bigger by the second. The sooner she left Wade's ranch, the sooner she could adjust to her new life. And he was right. She needed to buy supplies. It was time to get serious about this baby.

"Sorry about that." Wade shut the cabin door behind him.

"Must have been important."

Had she heard his conversation? He should confide in her about putting his ranch up for sale. Heat rushed up his neck. He wasn't ready. "Nothing major. What do you say we go buy some of the items on the list?"

"Are there any stores around here that carry this stuff?"

"We'll go to the city and find a super-center. Bound to have some of what you need. Get your shoes on."

"You mean we're going now?" Her forehead wrinkled in adorable consternation. "It's over an hour away."

"Yeah. Why? You have other plans or something?"

"Very funny. You know my only plans involve eating, napping and rocking on the front porch."

"Well, there you go. Looks like you have room in your schedule to shop."

"Fine. Let me put on my comfy shoes."

"I'll run back home, get the truck and pick you up in ten minutes."

After returning home, changing shirts, checking his wallet, and grabbing two bottles of water and a few snacks, he drove back to her cabin. She stood on the porch with her purse over her shoulder.

"Let me help you up," he said.

"I can do it."

"It's a tall step." He escorted her to the passenger side and boosted her up to the seat before shutting the door. Then he loped around to the driver's side. Soon the truck was kicking up dust on the way out.

A tiny smile played on her lips as she stared out her window. Her hand gently massaged her stomach. The image pinched his heart.

She was going to be a great mother.

As he turned onto the main road, his mind wandered back in time. He had snippets of memories of his mom. Sitting on her lap, watching cartoons together. She'd loved him. He knew she did. He might not remember much, but the feeling of acceptance remained.

And then one day, she'd disappeared.

Just another day. Most of it escaped his memory. He knew he'd been at the babysitter's place while his mother worked. He also remembered worrying when she didn't show up to get him that night. Or the next night. Had she forgotten about him? Stopped loving him? It wasn't long before he'd been sent to his first foster home.

His life hadn't been the same since.

His family ties had been severed that day. He didn't belong to anybody, and nobody belonged to him.

Still, he had friends. Good friends.

He glanced over at Kit. His best friend. Her eyes had closed.

*Good.* She needed the sleep. He drove the

rest of the way trying not to think about his mother, his childhood. He didn't know what tomorrow held for him. The present was all he really had.

"I don't need a wipe warmer. What does it even do?" Kit grimaced at the box Wade held. He'd been trying to convince her to buy things left and right, and she was losing her mind. One tiny baby did not need all this stuff. Or did it? She really didn't know. "How many times have I told you I'm on a budget?"

"You don't want to clean him with a cold wipe, do you?" He inspected the box and read the features out loud. "His little tushie will be frozen."

"Put it back." She scanned the shelves for useful items, like pacifiers, bibs and diaper cream.

Wade pushed the cart forward a few feet and selected something off the shelf.

"What is this?" Taking it from his hands,

she gave him her most long-suffering stare. "And why would I need it?"

"It's baby's first alarm clock. Look, it's a frog."

She raised her eyes to the ceiling and prayed for patience. "Wade…" She paused, adjusting her tone to not sound like a hag. "…the baby can't tell time."

"But it's a frog." He held it up and made a puppy dog face.

"I'm sticking to the essentials. A newborn doesn't need an alarm clock."

"Fine." Sighing, he put it back on the shelf.

They strolled through the rest of the aisle, adding anything she needed to the growing pile. He turned to the next one and threw a package of diapers into the cart.

"Wait. I need to check the prices and sizes."

"Sizes? You're telling me diapers aren't one size fits all?"

"They get bigger as the baby does."

He started reading the labels. "What's N? What's 3? How do you know what to buy?" He shook his head in dismay.

"I think N means newborn." She pulled a package off the shelf and read the back. "Yep. The sizes go up from there."

He tossed three packs of newborn diapers into the cart as if he was shooting basketballs.

"I'd better get some bigger ones, too. I've been told babies grow out of everything at the speed of light."

"I'll get 'em." He put a few packages of the larger diapers in the cart. "What's next? Let's go to the clothes. The little guy has to have some style."

Style? The child would likely be spitting up all over himself. And who would see him, anyway? She bit her tongue. At least Wade was enjoying himself. If she had to admit it, she was, too. All of this baby paraphernalia made her son feel real. And this aisle—the diapers and wipes one—smelled like babies. The best smell in the world.

"I'll meet you by the clothes in a minute. I'm grabbing some baby shampoo first."

"I'll go with you." He guided the cart and waited while she decided on shampoo, lotion and creams.

"All set." She turned and felt a sharp pain. "Oh!" She pressed the heel of her hand into her side and almost doubled over.

"What is it? What's wrong?"

"A cramp, I think." She winced, rubbing the spot. Slowly, the throbbing subsided.

"You need to get off your feet." His voice was hard. Before she knew what was happening, he'd swept her into his arms and started carrying her away from the cart.

"Wade! Put me down. I'm fine. I can walk." She lightly slapped his arm, his firm, muscular arm that seemed to have no problem hoisting her pregnant self and carrying her through a crowded shopping center.

"No." He strode down the main aisle to the front, where there was a fast-food sandwich shop. After carefully depositing her in a chair, he went to the counter and bought her a sub and a bottle of water. Then he set them in front of her and took the chair opposite. "Eat."

She took one look at his face, which could have been carved out of granite, and realized how worried he was about her.

"Wade…" she said softly, covering his hand with hers. "I'm okay. Really."

"You said cramps were bad." The words were clipped. His cheeks were drawn, his eyes sharp with concern.

"This wasn't that type of cramp. It was more like a charley horse in my side. Abdominal cramps are bad." She pointed to her stomach. "The ones gripping your belly. Those are the ones to worry about."

The muscle in his cheek flickered, and he looked to the side and shifted his jaw. Finally, he met her eyes. "I don't like seeing you in pain. The baby… Well, a cramp's a cramp."

His words pounded her heart, and the riot of emotions she'd dealt with all day flooded back. She covered her face with her hands and tried to slow it all down—her thoughts, impressions and whatever was going on with Wade. To have him care about her was so much more than she'd had with Cam.

Then she nodded, trying to figure out how to tell him what she was feeling. She'd never be able to put it in words.

"It means a lot to me. That you care." It sounded so lame. How could she explain?

"Good. Because I do." He visibly relaxed. "I care about you, too. I don't ever want to see you in pain, either."

"I'm not. You won't."

What did that mean? Either he thought he could avoid pain or hide it from her. Neither was realistic. But then, her growing feelings for him weren't, either. She unscrewed the bottle cap. Took a sip. Unwrapped the veggie sub. When she sank her teeth into the first bite, tears threatened to spill. She was getting too used to his thoughtfulness. When she moved to Casper—and she would be soon—she was going to be the loneliest girl on the planet.

It was time to emotionally distance herself from Wade. If only she knew how...

# Chapter Nine

Wade kept one eye on Kit as she mingled with the other ladies Saturday night. Nash and Amy had invited them and some close friends over for a barbecue. The week had passed by quickly. Too quickly. He'd spent most of it harvesting the first cut of hay on the ranch. Cutting, baling, hauling and stacking hay was hot, sweaty, exhausting work. And he'd relished every minute of it. It meant he'd be able to take care of his cattle this winter. Hopefully.

The couple Ray mentioned hadn't visited JPX Ranch yet, but they also hadn't visited Dudley Farms. Ray assured him they'd be out soon.

In the meantime, Kit hadn't mentioned any more cramps and seemed happy spending her days quietly on the ranch. But in the back of his mind, he kept replaying the scene at the shopping center. When she'd doubled over in pain, something inside him had snapped.

He hadn't had that sensation in years—the fear of permanently losing someone he loved. He'd almost forgotten how sharp it hurt, how helpless it made him feel. He never wanted to experience it again.

"Where are you at?" Nash jabbed an elbow into his side. "I just made fun of your hat and you didn't even hear me."

"What's wrong with my hat?" He took off his straw cowboy hat and inspected it. "Looks good to me."

"Yeah, if you want to look like a rodeo wannabe."

"Oh!" Clint and Marshall pointed at him, laughing.

"The only wannabe here is you. You call yourself a barbecue master? The sauce has too much vinegar." Wade loved ribbing the guys. They'd been doing it nonstop for years. He'd always been able to count on them, but he hadn't told them about his financial predicament. He wasn't ready to admit how badly he'd messed up.

"Too much vinegar?" Nash placed his hand against his chest, putting on the wounded show of a lifetime. "Check your taste buds. No one wants candy syrup covering their pork."

He ignored Nash and turned to Marshall. "You ready for the wedding?"

Marshall grinned. "I've been ready since Christmas Eve, when I popped the question."

"Only one week away, my friend. There's still time to change your mind." He slung his arm over Marshall's shoulders and playfully punched his biceps.

"Why would I do that? Ainsley's the best thing that's ever happened to me." He gazed at the group of ladies, lifted his can of Coke to the pretty blonde and nodded. Wade's eyes about popped out of his head. Every woman over there held a baby, including Kit.

"The quadruplets are getting spoiled." Raleigh, Marshall's brother-in-law, beamed a proud smile toward the ladies.

"Yeah, they're growing like weeds. I miss them." Marshall lived a few hours away from Sweet Dreams. He waved to his sister, Belle, who held one of the quadruplets. She lifted the baby's hand and pretended to wave back.

"I think Belle needs me." Raleigh strode away from the men, and Wade watched him take the baby from Belle. The man kissed the boy's cheek and held him high in the air.

It made Wade think of Kit's little boy and how great it would be to hold him high in the air, too.

He looked at his friends and felt like the odd man out. They'd all found women to share their lives with. None of them had ever thought they'd get married, let alone have kids. But here they were—happy. It was hard to believe he was the only bachelor left.

"I hope Ainsley and I have a bunch of kids, too." Marshall sounded wistful.

A month ago, Wade would have teased him, but now?

He watched the women laugh with each other and coo at the babies. The sight positively tied up his heartstrings. And he didn't think he possessed heartstrings.

He swiveled to face his friends and all three had matching sappy expressions on their faces.

"Okay, what happened to y'all?" One by one, he pointed to Marshall, Nash and Clint. "We used to talk about horses and bull riding and cattle. You're all making goo-goo eyes at a group of women and babies."

The three exchanged amused glances.

Nash clapped his hand on Wade's shoulder. "It's okay, buddy. You'll understand soon."

"What's that supposed to mean?" He jerked away from Nash's touch. Honestly, his friends were starting to get on his nerves. Acting like they were all in on some grand secret.

"We all see how you are with Kit." Nash

raised his eyebrows and cocked his head to the side.

"She's my friend. My best friend. That's it." He crossed his arms over his chest.

"It's a good start." Clint's tone was matter-of-fact.

"The woman *is* pregnant and alone." Marshall shrugged and opened his hands to make a point.

"Yeah, and her husband just died and she's moving to Casper."

"So…move with her," Marshall said.

He closed his eyes and counted to five. He was *not* moving to Casper. Why would that even be a suggestion? Were his friends going through some sort of newlywed frenzy?

"I'm not moving. My life is right here." He stamped his foot to make his point. But was it true? He very well could be moving. And soon. He didn't have much say in the matter.

"Won't do you much good if your heart's in Casper." Clint shook his head.

Since when did Clint have so much to say? He'd always been quiet. Didn't stick his nose where it didn't belong—one of his best qualities, in Wade's opinion. A quality the man should pick back up.

Marshall scuffed his boot against the patio stones. "I sure would hate to see you all worked up again if she remarries, though. You were a mess the first go-round."

"I was not all worked up when she married Cam."

The three men pretended to whistle, looking everywhere but at him.

"I wasn't." His voice rose. "And who's to say she'd get remarried? She'll have enough to deal with. I don't see her adding another husband to the mix."

"She's a beautiful woman. She's young, and she'll have a baby, Wade," Nash said. "Wake up to reality."

A burning sensation flashed through his chest. His stupid friends were stressing him out. Probably trying to give him a stroke.

Clint took a step closer to him. "You've been in love with her for a long time. This is your chance."

Wade shifted his jaw and stared out toward the stables. He hadn't been in love with Kit for a long time. He'd never been in love with her. Wasn't in love now.

He loved her...but not in a romantic, let's-get-married sense.

There was a difference. A big difference. His friends were too thickheaded to see it.

"Land won't keep you warm. It's just a ranch." Clint started making his way to the women, with Marshall and Nash joining him. Wade reluctantly followed them. As Nash put his arm around Amy and made cooing noises to the baby girl in her arms, Wade steered clear of his former friends—the traitors—to stand next to Kit.

She smiled up at him, the freckles on her nose making her look younger than she was. "Isn't he precious? This is Max."

He studied the boy with chubby cheeks, fuzzy hair and big brown eyes. The baby was pretty cute.

"Here." She held Max out to Wade. "Will you hold him for a minute? I have an itch."

"I don't know." He raised his palms and backed up a step. He'd rather scratch whatever itched her than hold a squirming child, although the boy seemed to be quiet.

"Come on. It'll only be a second." She thrust the baby into his arms.

The baby weighed about as much as the injured young fox he'd found in the meadow last fall. But the boy was squishier and more compact. With his hands under the child's armpits, Wade held him out a few inches from his body. What now?

"What are you doing?" Kit straightened. "Haven't you ever held a baby before?"

"No." He tried to hand him back to her, but she wagged her finger, her eyes sparkling. "Oh, no, you need to learn how to hold him. First of all, he's not a grenade ready to detonate. You can keep him close to your body. Tuck him to your chest. Like this." She adjusted the baby, who stared into Wade's eyes as if he was the most fascinating thing he'd ever seen. Wade grinned. To his surprise, the baby smiled back.

"Did you see that?" He widened his eyes. "He smiled at me."

"He's so adorable."

"He is, isn't he?" Wade scrunched his nose at the little fellow, while Kit sidled up next to them and played peekaboo. The baby giggled. Pure joy. "Do that again, Kit."

She did, and Max laughed, his entire body shaking in Wade's arms.

If this was what having a baby was like, he could see why his friends wanted one. He peeked at Kit, who was engrossed in entertaining the baby, and the bottom dropped out of his stomach.

She'd be doing this with her own baby in Casper. Without him.

Someone else would fall in love with her and snatch her up and raise her baby with her.

Could he handle losing her to another man a second time?

When he'd never really handled losing her the first time?

* * *

Kit bit into another chocolate chip cookie as Lexi crunched a carrot stick. Amy dropped a handful of potato chips onto a paper plate. Strings of lights overhead added a festive touch to the pole barn awning above where they sat. Belle and Raleigh had gone home to put the quadruplets to bed, and Marshall and Ainsley had left with them. The men were off to the side lighting a fire in the pit. Their guffaws and laughter traveled clear and loud.

All evening Kit had grown more and more comfortable with these women. They'd compared notes on their pregnancies, laughed at the sight of Nash in a Kiss the Cook apron and munched their way through a full spread of food.

She wanted to tell them about the baby's health problems, and she wanted to share the good news that the test indicated he wouldn't have special needs. But she hadn't gotten the guts to do it.

What was she afraid of, anyway?

Pity, for one. And how many times had she confided something painful to a female friend, only to immediately feel an emotional distance? She'd learned the hard way that not everyone could handle the truth.

But...

Did it mean she shouldn't try? She thought of Sandra Bixby. Some women were really good at being there through the tough times. Kit had called Sandra this week and talked for a long time.

"Oh, get this." Amy wiped her greasy fingers on a napkin. "Ruby informed me she wants to name the baby."

Lexi grinned. "What did she come up with?"

"Cinderella if it's a girl, and Kristoff if it's a boy."

"Kristoff?" Lexi asked. "Where did she come up with that?"

"The movie *Frozen*." Kit hadn't taught second grade for years for nothing. "Ruby must love Disney movies."

"Oh, she does." Amy nodded, smiling. "Honestly, I'm surprised she didn't suggest Sven. She adores that reindeer."

"So…are you letting her pick the name?" Lexi teased.

"Uh, no." She shook her head decisively. "It will be a group effort. Kit, have you started a list of names yet?"

She bit her lower lip. "I was waiting."

"For what?"

"Well…" The timing was right. It would be simple to tell them the reason she was waiting. Her palms grew sweaty. "I found out the baby has some health issues. He has a hole in his heart."

"Oh, no!" Lexi's jaw dropped.

"How horrible." Lines creased Amy's forehead.

And before Kit knew what was happening, both women had wrapped their arms around her in a group hug. When they'd hugged it out, they stayed close to Kit.

"The doctor was worried the hole might be caused by a genetic mutation, so they ran a few tests on the baby. Thankfully, I got the results back earlier this week, and they were negative. He still has the hole, but at least he doesn't have special needs, too."

A fat teardrop fell from Amy's eye onto her cheek. "I'm so sorry you're going through this, Kit. If there's anything we can do..." She wiped the tear away. "I'm such a blubbery mess lately—don't mind me."

Lexi reached over and squeezed Kit's hand. "Anything. Anything at all we can do. If you need a ride to the doctor or just need someone to talk to, we're here."

She tried to tamp down the tears pressing against her own eyes and failed. These women had welcomed her without questions or judgment, and now they were offering her so much more than she'd ever given another female friend.

It hit her how stingy she'd been with her friendship over the years. So afraid of getting hurt, she hadn't bothered to show up and try.

"We didn't mean to make you cry." Lexi's

lips wobbled and soon she, too, had tears rolling down her cheeks. "I feel so bad for you. You lost your husband, and now your baby has a hole in his heart. It seems really unfair. Your burden is too heavy."

Kit blinked, whisking away the tears and trying to pull herself together. "It isn't too heavy. Don't worry about me. God has held me through all of this, and He won't let me down. I was feeling much worse—depressed, really—the three weeks I had to wait for the test results to come in. Hearing the results were negative was a huge relief. I feel better than I have in a long time."

"Three weeks?" Amy exchanged a horrified glance with Lexi. "You mean to tell me you had to wait three weeks not knowing if your baby had special needs?"

Kit nodded.

They both surrounded her once more and wrapped her in their arms.

"What is going on in here?" Nash stood with his fists planted on his hips. "Why are you all cryin'?"

Kit looked at Amy and Lexi, and all three of them started laughing. And the laughs grew harder and louder until she was afraid they'd gone into full-blown hysteria. She didn't care. It felt so good to laugh and to share her troubles.

"Come on." Nash took Amy's hand and led her toward the bonfire. "You need a marshmallow. I don't like seeing you cry."

"You okay?" Clint slid his arm around Lexi's waist and placed his other hand on her small tummy. She nodded, and they strolled away to the fire, where chairs and bales of hay had been lined up for seats.

Which left Wade. Alone. With her. In all his masculine glory. He took three steps forward. His eyes blazed with intensity. She waited for him to say something. To ask her why she was upset. To try and force her to get off her feet and sit for a while.

He did none of those things.

Face-to-face, under those pretty stringed lights, he cupped her cheeks in his hands. Emotions ran through those blue eyes faster than wild horses pounding across the prairie. Then only one remained. She sucked in a breath.

He'd never looked at her this way before. With need and fire and...more. Her insides warmed, her knees grew weak and anticipation palpitated in the air between them. She could feel his breath as he leaned in. His hands snaked behind her back, and he urged her to him, never breaking eye contact.

When his lips touched hers, she flew back in time, back to when she'd been a little girl and adored him with every ounce of energy she had. When his mouth pressed more firmly, she was reminded she was all woman now. And she gave in to a lifetime of longing and kissed him back.

She spiraled into sensations—the cedarwood scent of his cologne, the hint of lemonade on his lips, the contained muscular strength holding her as if she was valuable, a prize.

She'd waited her entire life for this moment, and she hadn't even known it.

His hands caressed her lower back in circular motions. She touched the back of his neck, sinking her fingers into his cropped hair. The kiss went on until the baby made his presence known.

Wade jerked back. "Did you feel that?"

"Of course I felt it." She kept her arms around his neck. The baby kicked again. His movements were getting stronger. Each little jolt added to her hope of keeping him alive.

Wade shifted his hands and his attention to her belly. Another movement. He flashed her a surprised grin. No words were needed.

His face fell. What went on in that mind of his? He wasn't going to apologize for kissing her, was he?

"A part of me feels like an imposter." He tucked a lock of her hair behind her ear. "Cam should have been here for this. He should have been the one to take you shopping, pamper you, feel the baby kick. I know things were bad and all, but are you missing him?"

Wait…what? One minute he was kissing

her with so much emotion her head was still spinning, and now he wanted to talk about her dead husband?

"No, I'm not. He wouldn't have been here for this." She dropped her hands to her sides. "I told you. He wanted a divorce."

"But the baby…it would have changed his mind."

"Nothing would have changed his mind. Trust me."

Wade's expression softened. "Why did he want a divorce?"

She'd been staying with Wade for almost three weeks. Two weeks ago in Casper, she'd told him Cam wanted a divorce. He hadn't asked for details. Why did he want them now?

"It doesn't matter." She brushed past him, but he caught her arm.

"It does to me."

"Leave it alone." She wanted one night to bask in feeling special. The second she told Wade that Cam had cheated on her not once but three times, he'd wonder why, and he'd come up with the truth.

She hadn't been enough for Cam.

She'd never be enough for Wade, either.

Why would any man blessed enough to be married to Kit throw his marriage away? Wade leaned against the railing on his porch later that night. He couldn't sleep. The stars twinkled brightly above, and every now and then a shooting star would streak through the inky sky. In the distance, coyotes howled.

Things had changed tonight.

He didn't like change. Not this kind, anyway.

He blamed it on his so-called friends. All their talk about families and Kit and her getting remarried had discombobulated him. Was *discombobulated* a word? He didn't know. Or care. Something had shaken him up and left him disoriented.

He'd tried too many new things tonight.

Holding a baby. And liking it.

Seeing Kit surrounded by women he admired. Thinking the three of them laughing and crying and being pregnant looked right.

Watching his buddies pair off with their pregnant wives. Wanting to be paired off with a pregnant wife, too.

He slapped his thigh. That was the problem. He couldn't go on pretending he was right for the role. He didn't have it in him to offer her or any woman forever. Not when forever could be as short as his mother's.

And then he'd gone and kissed her—kissed Kit. He raised his eyes to the highest star and shook his head.

It had been a good kiss.

A real good kiss.

A knock-your-boots-off, never-let-it-end kiss.

He had half a mind to march down the lane and wake her up just to kiss her again.

He could not kiss her again.

Even if she had tasted like chocolate cookies and home. He'd been about to get carried away—and wasn't he a little old to get so caught up in a kiss?—when the baby had kicked. Feeling that little nudge to his abdomen had been about the coolest thing he'd ever experienced.

He dropped his face into his hands. What was he doing?

*You've been in love with her for a long time. This is your chance.*

Since when had Clint become the expert on Wade's love life?

He didn't have a love life. Wouldn't have one.

Clint was wrong. He hadn't been in love with Kit for a long time, and he wasn't now.

He wasn't in love, period.

He puffed out his cheeks and exhaled. Life had been easier when Kit belonged to Cam. Maybe they were divorcing because they hadn't been compatible. Or they'd grown apart. One of them could have cheated.

Not Kit.

He didn't see her breaking her vows. Loyal to a fault. At times she'd clung to people who weren't good for her, and he'd wanted to tear her away for her own good. But he never had.

He'd been torn away from too many people in his own life to ever insert himself that way in hers. And, if he were brutally honest with himself, she was one of the few people he couldn't lose. He just couldn't.

Jeopardizing their relationship with illusions of love wasn't going to happen no matter what his friends said.

## Chapter Ten

She was too aware of him in church Sunday morning. Wade smelled clean and woodsy, and he was wearing dark jeans and a crisp white button-down with the sleeves rolled up. Corded forearms flexed as he held open the hymn book. They sang along with the congregation. His low voice was so inviting, Kit had to discreetly scoot away to create an inch of space between them. She needed to create more than an inch—more like a couple hundred miles. And even that might not be enough.

For hours she'd tried to sleep, only to repeatedly replay his kiss in her mind. Had she been grinning like an idiot in her super-comfortable bed half the night? Yes. And worse, she'd let her mind wander to places it shouldn't go.

Like staying in Sweet Dreams and raising the baby here. On Wade's ranch. With Wade.

Unfortunately, her mind was still stuck in that fantasy, and his presence next to her wasn't helping matters. Had the air-conditioning broken or something? She fanned her face.

"You all right?" Wade whispered.

No, she was not all right. She'd foolishly left herself open to more heartbreak and pain. Wade didn't love her. Sure, he'd been taking care of her. Yeah, last night he'd kissed her. What a kiss...

But a spur-of-the-moment kiss didn't equal love.

And one loveless marriage was enough for her for a lifetime.

"I'm fine, thanks." She wasn't what Wade needed, anyhow. He needed a wife who was fully present. One without a bunch of baggage from her past. Someone fun who challenged him. Someone beautiful and kind. Someone who would make him happy, not disappoint him the way she had Cam.

As much as she loathed the thought of moving in to the apartment in Casper, her move-in date was fast approaching, and her doctors' appointments were less than two weeks away.

She had to get her head out of fantasyland and into reality, where it belonged. Wade's friend Marshall was getting married on Saturday, and Wade was a groomsman. That meant Friday night he'd be at the rehearsal dinner and all day Saturday at the wedding. Marshall and Ainsley had invited her to both. She planned on attending. It would be her last hoorah in Sweet Dreams.

Disappointment made her slump.

She'd come back and visit. After the baby was born and things had settled. She'd been getting better at pushing away worries about his health lately. A big part of that was due to Wade.

It was okay to rely on him as a friend.

It wasn't okay to mentally make him something more.

"In the second book of Corinthians we're told we have a merciful God, the source of all comfort. As you prepare for a new week, remember His mercy, acknowledge His comfort. Amen." The pastor signaled for them to rise.

Kit placed her program on the seat next to her and pushed her hands against the pew to stand. She was getting more off balance as her belly grew. Wade grasped her elbow and helped her up the rest of the way.

She would miss his touch when she moved. She'd forgotten how a simple touch could make her feel less alone in this world.

Life with Cam had been very lonely.

Her world would be changing soon. New roles, new town, new everything. At least she could rest in the assurance that God would see her through it all.

When the service ended, she and Wade

made their way outside to the lawn, where groups of people chatted.

"Do you mind if we skip breakfast at Dottie's this morning?" he asked.

"Not at all. Why?"

"I need to check on a section of fence, and it will take a while."

Disappointment spilled to her toes. She propped up what she hoped was a bright smile. "No problem. I think I'll take a nap. And I might do a little online shopping for the new apartment."

Something flickered in his eyes, but she ignored it. This was what they were doing, right? Reminding each other last night's kiss hadn't meant a thing and they both had their own lives. Apart from each other. With no kissing or commitment allowed.

"Kit!" Amy hustled over with pink cheeks glowing and dark brown hair swinging behind her. "I talked to my mom this morning, and we want to come down and help you out when you have the baby. We'll stay in a hotel for a few days until you're on your feet."

Amy's eyes sparkled with excitement. This woman—this virtual stranger—wanted to help. And her mother did, too. How amazing was that?

"I would love that." Kit took Amy's hands in hers and squeezed them. "But if it's too much or something comes up, I understand. I'll be fine."

"Nonsense. It will give me a crash course on newborns. And, trust me, you want my mom helping. She knows what she's doing and doesn't get frazzled."

A mom helping her—how bittersweet. She had no memories of her own mother. Aunt Martha had been a nightmare. The foster homes had been fine mostly, but as time wore on and she moved again and again, her heart had crusted over. As much as she'd wanted a mother, she'd given up hope. She'd resigned herself to the fact she was alone. Then Cam came along and she'd thought her circumstances had changed, but they hadn't. Not really.

And now she had two women offering to help her when the baby arrived...

Wade cleared his throat. She'd forgotten he was there. He didn't look happy.

"Sorry. I know you're busy. We can go." She patted his arm, then turned to Amy. "Thanks again. And thank your mom for me."

"I wish you'd stay here for good." Amy hugged her.

"I have to do what's best for the baby." She waved goodbye. Wade put his hand against the small of her back to direct her to the parking lot.

The baby. Best for the baby. An NICU. Good doctors. Proximity to the hospital.

What if the hole healed on its own? Or what if the doctors were able to surgically correct it after she gave birth?

Would she really need to live in Casper?

If the baby's health improved, she could live wherever she wanted. Even Sweet Dreams. What a comforting thought. But could she

live near Wade and not fall in love with him?
When she was already halfway there?

Wade didn't need to check on fence, and
he could have gone to Dottie's Diner with
his friends, but he'd chickened out. The more
time he spent with the other couples, the
more he wanted to be part of one, too. And
sitting next to Kit in church this morning
had been pure torture.

She'd smelled like tropical flowers. Her
warm skin kept brushing his, making him
all too aware of her beauty. Now that he
knew exactly how she fitted in his arms and
how her lips felt against his, he could think
of little else. So he'd made an excuse to get
away from her, from his friends, from everything.

He needed to create some major distance
between himself and Kit.

He steered his truck south to the hundred
acres that had started it all. The weather was
perfect. Sunny and not too windy.

And while he was driving to inspect fence

that didn't need inspecting, Kit was back at the ranch shopping for the apartment he'd been avoiding thinking about. The unsafe apartment he couldn't bear to think of her living in.

He turned up the radio's volume and let the country song chase away his thoughts. Before long he pulled onto the long dirt road leading to the old house, aka the shack. He drove past it to where the pasture began.

Stopping at the gate, he got out and just stood and watched the cattle. Tails flicking, heads bowed to forage the grass.

His cell phone rang, and without checking the caller, he answered.

"The young couple I told you about wants to tour your ranch. Today." Ray Simon sounded excited.

His heart sank. "They haven't checked out Dudley Farms, have they?"

"No. I've pushed it hard. Told their agent you're motivated to sell. They aren't very interested in it. But they definitely want to see JPX Ranch. They can be there in two hours. Are you okay with that?"

Was he okay with selling his home, the inheritance from a man who had given him the rights of a son?

He'd never be okay with it.

But what choice did he have?

"Yeah."

"I'll call their agent and tell them. Hopefully, we'll get an offer soon."

"Got it. I'm out at another property right now."

"That's fine. Their agent can call me with any questions." Ray went over a few more things before hanging up.

Wade slipped his phone back in his pocket and hitched a cowboy boot on the bottom rail of the fence to watch the cattle graze. *How did I get here? How did I go from top of the world, more money than I knew what to do with, to this? I can't believe I might lose JPX.*

If the couple bought JPX Ranch, where would that leave him?

Back to where he'd started. Except with more money in his pocket.

Slowly, he turned and surveyed the land. He would still own this. His original ranch wasn't part of the property for sale. Moving back into the shack would be the ultimate humiliation after finding so much success.

Or he could move to Dudley Farms.

It had been months since he'd been there. He could barely remember the house, since he'd been interested only in the land. He should head up there soon even if the thought of living there, far away from his friends, didn't appeal in the slightest.

Maybe it was better Kit was moving soon. She wouldn't be around to see his fall from grace. With her in another town, he'd forget about the kiss, and he'd figure out how to move forward with or without JPX Ranch. He'd be fine. And so would she. She had Amy and Amy's mom to help her when the baby came. She wouldn't need him anymore.

But he needed her.

Gritting his teeth, he clenched his hands

into fists. He'd better get her away from the ranch while the couple toured it or he'd have a lot of explaining to do.

"I've got some good news." Kit scooped coleslaw onto her fork at Roscoe's BBQ late that afternoon. It wasn't really good news, but Wade didn't need to know that. She'd been surprised when he'd shown up this afternoon insisting they go into Sweet Dreams for some shopping and dinner. After smelling all the candles in Loraine's Mercantile, they'd window-shopped on Main Street. An awkwardness existed between them that hadn't been there before. She figured her news would help distract both of them from the inconvenient feelings surrounding them. "I can move in to the apartment a few days early."

He stared at her for a charged moment, then resumed chewing his pulled-pork sandwich.

"I'm going there Wednesday morning to do a walk-through and to sign the final pa-

perwork. I can move in as early as Friday."
She ripped a hunk off her biscuit, but didn't
eat it.

"I thought you were going with me to the
rehearsal dinner. And what about the wedding on Saturday?"

"I'll still go to both." She was glad he still
wanted her to go with him. "I'll move next
Monday. It will be nice to spend one more
weekend here."

"You can spend more than a weekend, you
know."

"I know." She frowned, staring at her
plate. "It's time to go, though."

"Line up a few other apartments." He
didn't look happy, and the words were gruff.
"I'll take you on Wednesday."

"You don't have to go with me."

"I want to. I'll drive." He avoided eye contact. "I've been wanting to check on Dudley Farms, anyhow. We'll swing up on the
way back."

"I'd like to see it." She took another bite.
"If you don't want to drive to Casper, don't

worry about it. I'll be fine going there on my own."

"I'm not leaving you to do this by yourself."

Just the words she'd gotten used to hearing. The ones she relied on from him more than he knew.

He frowned, rubbing his chin. "Will it be too much for you? Sitting in the truck for hours can't be good for you or the baby."

"It's not as though we'd be driving all day."

He considered it and nodded. "Okay. But if at any point you don't feel right, you let me know and we'll stop and rest. I don't want you overdoing it or getting blood clots in your legs from sitting too long."

Blood clots? She fought the urge to smile. The man got more paranoid every minute. And she didn't mind it at all. It was nice to have him care. She didn't know what she'd do without him to lean on.

Casper already seemed like the loneliest place in the world.

She glanced at his lips and quickly looked away. Her neck grew warm.

His question from last night roared back— *Why did Cam want a divorce?*

Because something was lacking in her that other people had. No one ever chose her, wanted her, and Cam had obviously realized he'd made a mistake.

"And I'm serious about the other apartments, Kit. I don't like the looks of the one you're renting."

She didn't like the looks of it, either. But she didn't have other options. Cam's life insurance would pay for the baby's doctor bills and her living expenses until she found a job. She couldn't blow it all on a fancy apartment. Even if the one she'd lined up did give her the creeps.

"It will be okay." But would it? How many times had she told herself those words? How many times had it *not* been okay? She didn't know what else to do, though. No job equaled no lease unless someone cosigned for it. And she'd never ask Wade to do that.

She excused herself and hurried to the bathroom.

She stared at her reflection in the mirror. Her face had filled out as the pregnancy progressed. The freckles on her nose blended with the tan she'd picked up since moving here. She looked healthier than she had in a long time.

*Cam, if you hadn't died, I wouldn't be forced to live in a rat's nest of an apartment.*

Closing her eyes, she took a deep breath.

Actually, she'd still be stuck in a crummy apartment. She'd still be alone, desperate for her baby to be okay.

How many times had she stared into a mirror and seen this exact face—the one with hope etched in the forehead—only to shed devastated tears?

She kept telling herself she was over Cam. She kept trying not to be angry at him. He was dead, after all. But the anger flared again and again.

*God, please help me to forgive him for real.*

Her thoughts went to Wade and the million and one ways he'd taken care of her since she'd arrived. Maybe that was the problem. Wade's natural appealing attributes only highlighted Cam's lack of them.

A soft knock on the door had her scrambling to get herself together.

"Are you all right?" Wade's voice carried through the door.

Was she all right? She didn't know.

"Kit?" His voice grew firm, concerned.

She opened the door. "I'm fine." She moved forward, but he stood his ground, searching her face for...something. She hoped he didn't find whatever he was looking for.

"What's going on with you?" He took her biceps in his hands, caressing them gently.

"Nothing." She tried to smile. Knew she failed.

"Is this about last night? Me kissing you?"

Was it?

*Yes.*

But not in the way he thought. Wade made her feel cherished, cared for—important—in ways Cam hadn't. Which was worse? Being married to a man who lavished affection on other women? Or getting affection from a man who might not ever want marriage?

"Kit…" He used his talk-to-me tone.

*Fine.* He wanted her to talk? She'd tell him what she'd been keeping in. Maybe then she could move on from Cam's death and from whatever was going on here. She could slink off to Casper and build a new life.

"I'm not talking in the bathroom." She gave his chest a light shove. He cocked an eyebrow and moved aside for her to go past him.

They returned to the table.

She didn't even pretend to eat. "Last night you wanted to know why Cam asked for a divorce."

His eyes flickered in surprise.

"Our marriage wasn't the stuff of fairy

tales and happy endings." She forced herself to maintain eye contact. "It started out fine, like most couples', I suppose. But within a few months, Cam got restless. I liked quiet nights at home. He liked hanging out with his buddies."

She scooted her chair back slightly to rest her hands on her stomach.

"What happened?" Wade asked.

"At first I was hurt. Then I got vocal about his nights out. He didn't like that. The more I wanted him home, the less he stuck around. We pretty much stopped talking to each other."

If she'd made more of an effort with him, would he have stayed faithful?

"He was an idiot." Wade shook his head in disgust.

The corner of her mouth lifted, but she shrugged. "Looking back, I'm not sure why I was so surprised to find out he'd cheated on me."

"He cheated on you?"

She lifted three fingers. "Three times."

His face screwed up as he mulled it over. "Why did you stay?"

"I still wanted it...you know...the perfect family. I thought he'd change."

"But he didn't."

"No, and I couldn't see a different future. So I stayed." Would she have done anything differently? Left him after the first affair? Pushed harder for counseling? Gone out with him instead of staying home? All the options were giving her a headache.

"What happened? You said he asked for a divorce. What changed?"

Her lungs seized up. This was what she'd been avoiding for months. *What changed?*

"I guess he finally realized I didn't make him happy." Saying the words out loud hurt. "He'd found someone who did, and he wanted to be with her." A lump grew in Kit's throat, and she swallowed, but it had lodged in tight.

"Is that what you believe?" His baby blues held no judgment. No pity. Just raw honesty.

She shrugged. *Of course that's what I be-*

*lieve! What else could I think? I bored my husband. Our life didn't satisfy him. And he wanted out.*

"I'm sorry, Kit. You didn't deserve that."

The lump expanded. She would not cry. She balled her hands into fists to keep from falling apart.

"Do you still love him?" Wade asked.

Did she? No. What did it say about her? She'd vowed to love him until death. She'd stopped loving him long before then. She wasn't going to sugarcoat it with Wade. He could handle the truth. If he thought less of her, so be it.

"No, I don't love him. I tried, but I didn't try hard enough. I haven't loved Cam for a long time."

He nodded and stared into space. "Did you ever love him?"

"Yes, I did." She'd loved him. He just hadn't loved her. Not enough, anyhow. And maybe she hadn't loved him enough, either.

Maybe she wasn't capable of loving anyone enough.

She refused to believe it. That was one lie she would not buy into. Not today. Not ever. She could love as fiercely as anyone.

# Chapter Eleven

She could not see herself living here.

Kit scrunched her nose at the scratched and chipped laminate countertop in the kitchen of the apartment Wednesday morning. The dark kitchen had worn cabinets, old appliances and pea-green linoleum floors bubbling in spots. A fluorescent light overhead made sizzling sounds and flickered now and then. In the small living room, the carpet was worn and stained. Ditto in the dining area to the right. She wouldn't think about the furniture the apartment came with. The orange-and-brown-plaid couch had seen better days. The faux leather armchair had, too.

A hallway led to two small bedrooms and a bathroom with a stained sink and dirty tub.

She pushed away her disgust. For the first time she regretted selling all her furniture. At the time she'd convinced herself she never wanted to see it again. She'd thought it would only bring bad memories.

But this apartment…was one bad memory waiting to happen.

Wade hadn't said a word. His locked jaw and the muscle flexing in his cheek said it all. He opened the window overlooking the shared balcony. Deafening rap music flooded the room. He slammed it shut with a thud.

"You can't be serious, Kit." His voice trailed off to a low growl.

She wanted to cry, to run screaming from the place, or at the very least, curl into the fetal position until the apartment morphed into something livable. But she held her head high.

"It will be fine." A worse lie had never crossed her lips.

"Let's take this—" he nudged the edge of the couch with the tip of his cowboy boot "—atrocity of furniture out of the equation. It's a bedbug hotel if I've ever seen one. There are too many rough characters out front, it's too noisy and…" He faced her, crossing his arms over his chest. "I can't let you do this."

"You're not letting me do anything." She kept her tone light and breezy, but she was this close to falling into his arms and begging him to take her anywhere but here.

"Where is all your stuff going to fit?" He stepped back, a glazed look of horror in his eyes.

"I don't have any. I thought I told you. I sold it all."

"Why?" He inhaled deeply, made a sour face and appeared ready to gag. Kit didn't blame him. There was an odd smell in this room.

"Easier that way." She hated the memories her old furniture brought up.

"You can't use this furniture. You'll get hepatitis. Or tapeworm. Or both."

"I'll cover it with a sheet." She eyed the couch warily. Wade had a point.

"Kit...don't do this." He reached over and took her hand in his.

She waited for him to say more. Held her breath, hoping he would say the words she wanted to hear. Give her a reason to come up with a new plan for her and the baby. But his silence said it all.

*Stupid, really.* What did she think? He suddenly had feelings for her? After her confession about Cam's other women and not making him happy? That really clinched it for her, for sure.

Wade's eyes seared into her. And she caught her breath.

*I love him.*

Of all the terrible places she could have that little revelation, this apartment was the worst.

*I love him, and I want him to love me,*

*to say I would make him happy. That I'm enough, I've always been enough for him.*

She'd never really been enough for anyone. No one had ever adopted her. She'd been shuffled from home to home. Cam was the first person who'd chosen her. *Her.* And yet the relationship had ended the same—with her not enough.

Her baby would *never* feel that way.

He would feel wanted and important. Every day of his life.

Which was why she would make this nasty apartment work. It was affordable. It allowed her to stay home with him and pay for any treatments he needed. The stinky couch and lumpy mattress on the bed would be a blessing.

"No. No way. We're leaving. End of story." Wade's wide stance and hands on his hips meant business. Didn't he get it? She *had* to make this work. She'd reached the end of her tether.

"I'm out of options, okay, Wade?" She ran her hand over her hair.

"Then I'll cosign and put the money down myself." The muscle in his cheek pulsed.

"I can't let you do that."

"You can. Do you really think it's safe here for you or the baby?" He shook his head. "I can't let you move in to this crime scene waiting to happen. I just can't. You know what happened to my mother. A few years ago, I drove past the address where we lived. It wasn't this town, but it might as well have been. Same run-down neighborhood. Same questionable tenants hanging around. Look at what happened to her."

Kit hung her head. Thinking about Wade's young mother kidnapped and murdered always bothered her. Glancing up, she met his eyes. They pleaded with her.

*Okay, Lord, I can't put him through the worry. I won't. But I'm not taking his money, either. If he's generous enough to cosign for me, help me find a better apartment and a way to pay for the rent all year.*

"You win," she said softly. "I appreciate

you cosigning for me, but I will cover any money that needs to be put down."

His face cleared and he swept his arm to the door. "Let's get out of here and never come back."

"What about my deposit?"

"We'll talk to the landlord on the way out."

An hour later, Kit relaxed as she trailed her finger across the countertop in a bright kitchen with white cabinets, tile floors and white appliances. She would love to bring her baby home to this pretty place. The master bedroom even had a walk-in closet and an attached half bath. Wade had negotiated to get half her deposit back from the other place, which was more than she'd hoped.

"What do you think?" Wade leaned his elbows on the counter. The building was part of a larger complex, and it was tucked back away from the main road.

The rent was more than the other apartment, but, since it was the garden level, not as much as she thought it would be. If she kept her other expenses low, she'd be okay. "Quiet. Roomy. I like it."

"The couches and furniture are in good shape." Wade rapped his knuckles on the counter. "I like that it has covered parking."

"I do, too. I'm putting a deposit down." She snapped a few pictures, then slid the phone back in her purse. She'd need to buy baby furniture. Soon. For the first time, the thought made her smile.

He locked the door on their way out and drove the short distance to the manager's office. As Kit filled out the paperwork, Wade sat stiffly in the chair next to her.

When she finished, she slid the papers to Wade. He scrawled his name on them and handed them back to the manager.

"When can I move in?"

"I'll check both your credit reports now. If they come back okay, you can move in anytime after Friday." The woman scanned them and glanced up at her. "I'll need first and last months' rent today."

Kit reached for her checkbook. A hand on hers had her looking up.

"Are you sure about moving here?" Wade's eyes gleamed. "You can stay on the ranch."

She attempted to smile to reassure him. "I've got doctors' appointments lined up, and I need to get my life together."

"I can take you to the appointments."

Every word out of his mouth was a temptation. *I could stay. Wade would take me to the appointments. Nothing has to change...*

But she loved him.

Which meant everything already had changed. She was just delaying the inevitable.

"It's time for me to get settled." She cared about him too much to flirt with disaster anymore. Her fingers trembled as she wrote out the check and ripped it off. Sliding it to the manager, she couldn't help feeling like a chapter of her life had ended. A good chapter.

Would the next be tragic? Or wonderful?

It was time to find out.

* * *

Wade turned into the drive leading to Dudley Farms. He'd taken Kit out to lunch after signing the lease, and they'd driven in silence for over an hour. He didn't know what to think, but whatever it was, he couldn't help feeling his life was slipping through his hands. He'd come this close to telling her he cared too much about her to let her leave. And next thing he knew, he was cosigning for an apartment.

It had been the right thing to do.

He wanted to tell her about having the ranch up for sale, but he would have to admit the truth about his finances. He wasn't ready.

It dumbfounded him how much having money really did change things. A year ago, he would have taken one look at the filthy apartment, escorted her to his truck and told her he was finding her a new apartment and paying for it himself. He would have found the biggest, brightest, safest, nicest place there was. Somewhere she'd be happy.

Speaking of happy…

He hadn't been able to chase away the thoughts that had been racing around in his head since their conversation Sunday night at Roscoe's BBQ.

Cam had cheated on her.

And she believed it was because she didn't make him happy.

Any man blessed enough to spend even two minutes with Kit would be the happiest man alive.

He tried to shift his attention to the land splayed before him, but he couldn't concentrate. Not with Kit moving in a few days. Not when she'd admitted she'd stopped loving Cam long ago. Not when Wade couldn't bear to think about her not being around. Not with this weight pressing down on his heart.

"It's beautiful." Kit pointed out the window. "No wonder you bought it. I can see the river winding through the land from here. And look at all those pines in the distance. I'm surprised you're willing to sell it."

It was beautiful, and he didn't care. He never should have bought it. It was the source of all his problems right now. If he didn't own it, he could pay for Kit's baby's medical bills and buy her all the baby supplies she'd ever need. He could resume the life he'd enjoyed all these years on JPX Ranch. Instead, his hope was drying up.

The couple who'd toured the ranch last weekend hadn't made an offer on it.

If he could sell one of his properties, he'd have the cash he was accustomed to. There would be no more selling horses and equipment. Paying off the loans and having JPX's income streaming in would allow him to live exactly the way he had before.

Only this time, he wouldn't get greedy. He'd be content with what he had.

*God, just give me another chance. Please. Find a buyer.*

The truck hit a bump as the main house came into view. The massive log home sat on a hill. He knew it was empty, and he was preparing to drive past it to check the stables, but an SUV was parked out front.

"That's strange. I wonder who's here." He

jumped down from the truck and went to the passenger side to help Kit down. Her hand in his was small, delicate. He wanted to hold on to it forever.

He guided her up to the front door. It took a few minutes to find his key. Just when he was inserting the key into the lock, he heard footsteps approach from inside. The door swung open, and a short, balding man with brown eyes and a serious expression appeared. "You'll have to come back. I'm showing the property now."

"Oh, I didn't realize." Wade hadn't expected to see a real estate agent here. "I'm Wade Croft. I own Dudley Farms."

"Joe Selina." His face transformed with a big smile. "My clients are upstairs." Then he addressed Kit. "I'll get out of the way so you can get off your feet, dear."

Wade followed Kit inside.

She turned to him. "Will you point me to the powder room?" He pointed down the hall.

Joe beamed at Wade. "Congratulations."

"What do you mean?" Were the clients he mentioned ready to make an offer? The sheer relief of the thought almost made him stagger.

"The baby. Hard to believe you're willing to sell this place. It's good land to raise a family."

The clicking of footsteps on the staircase in the large foyer had them both looking up. A middle-aged couple, both wearing short-sleeved shirts, jeans and cowboy boots, chatted on the way down.

"Red and Tori, I have a nice surprise for you. The owner of Dudley Farms, Wade Croft, is here with his beautiful bride. He might be able to answer some of those questions from earlier."

His beautiful bride? A wave of longing hit him hard. "Actually, Kit's an old friend visiting from out of town." He shook Red's hand when the man reached the bottom, and greeted Tori. Red asked Wade a few questions about the house, and Wade did his best to answer them.

Kit returned from the bathroom, and Tori zoomed over to her.

"I'm ready to take a short break, Red," Tori said. "Why don't you and Joe check out the barns without me? I'd rather relax a spell here."

"She doesn't care much for stuffy outbuildings on a day like today." Red chuckled.

"I don't mind barns, but you'll want to look at every piece of equipment out there. I know you."

"You say that like it's a bad thing. I've got to know what I'm getting myself into, T." He scratched his chin thoughtfully.

"Yeah, and I reckon you're familiar with every tool and tractor in Wyoming at this point."

"I want to inspect the fields, too." Red eyed Wade for a moment longer than necessary. "You coming with us?"

He wanted to. Wanted to do anything he could to sell this land.

But Kit...

"I'm sorry, but I'd better pass." He glanced over at her, and she waved him off.

"Go, Wade. I'm fine. I'll stay with Tori. Looks like there are some loungers out on the deck. I could use a little time-out from the truck."

"Excuse us a moment." He escorted her to the massive living room, where they could talk in private. "Are you sure? This will take a while. Probably a few hours. We can drive home. I don't want—"

"Go. You might not have this chance again. Who knows? God might have set this meeting up." She patted his arm and smiled.

Had God set this in motion? Did God care about him that much? When Wade so rarely relied on Him? Prayers weren't answered *that* quickly, were they?

"Thank you." He planted a kiss on her temple. "Text me if you need me."

He returned to the foyer. "I'm ready when you are."

Joe and Red grinned, and Tori waved Kit over. "Let's sit on this deck, honey. It's nice and shady. My kids would love it here. They're grown now, but I have a hard time not picturing them young..."

Wade led the way out of the house. "I haven't owned this spread for long, but I'll try to answer any questions you might have."

Red climbed into the passenger seat. "I appreciate it. The house meets Tori's standards. There's no mistaking this is beautiful land. I miss farming. But there are a few things nagging at me."

Wade started the engine, waited for Joe to settle into the back seat, and drove down the long lane to the stables. He didn't like leaving Kit by herself with Tori, even though the woman had seemed nice. He hadn't brought her out here just to abandon her.

Why *had* he brought her out here?

He could have come by himself next week. But more and more, he'd been wanting to tell her the truth about his finances. He was tired of carrying this burden around. Coming out here, seeing the land, well, he needed to decide if he could make a life here. Get closure. Help him accept that if his ranch sold, this might be his new home.

See what she thought about the idea.

After parking the truck, Wade hopped out and described the various outbuildings. They went through each structure, examining everything from tractors to the tack room. As Red peppered Wade with questions, Wade was surprised to have answers for most of them. Maybe he knew more about farming than he'd given himself credit for.

"You okay with riding horseback?" He jerked his thumb to the horses nearby.

"Wouldn't want to see the fields any other way." Red grinned. Joe nodded his approval.

Several minutes later, the three of them headed out. Wade showed Red the river and empty pastures. As he looked around, he was proud to see the ranch held rich natural resources and a charm all its own. Maybe Red would appreciate it and want to buy it.

They moved on to the farmland.

"See, this is what's been nagging me." Red pointed to the weeds and meadow where the crops should have been. "This is fertile ground. I noticed the irrigation equipment. You have water rights. Why aren't there any crops?"

His failure had just been named. He had no choice but to tell Red the truth.

"The irrigation equipment is old and doesn't work. Last summer was dry, if you recall. I bought this land with the intention of farming it. My funds got low, I couldn't afford to repair the equipment and last year's crops never materialized. I opted not to plant seed this year."

Red chewed on the thought.

"It *is* good farmland, though," Joe piped up. "I've got the previous owner's stats in the file."

"Joe here tells me you have another ranch for sale, as well." Red narrowed his eyes. "Why is that?"

He'd thought about his mistake so many times, but until now, he hadn't said it out loud. It was time to own up to it even if it revealed his weakness.

"To buy this property, I had to put my ranch up as collateral."

"Ah." Red's face cleared. "And you need to get the loan taken care of, huh?"

As much as it pained him, he needed to give Red an honest assessment of both properties. "My ranch is on the other side of the Bighorn Mountains. It's near the little town of Sweet Dreams. The price on it is higher, but it's got more to offer. Newly renovated house and cabins. Cattle. Grazing land galore. If you're not sold on Dudley Farms, come out and take a look at JPX Ranch."

"I might. I'll talk to Tori about it. But I have a question for you first."

"Go ahead." He braced himself.

"What do you plan on doing if we buy the land we're on now?"

The future spread out before him so bright, so familiar, it was like the sun suddenly appearing after days of rain. "I'll stick with ranching on JPX. I never should have expanded in the first place. I'm a rancher, not a farmer."

"And if we come out to JPX and love it? What will you do then?"

He could feel his face falling, but he firmed his chin. "I'll move out here and make a go of it."

"You'd be happier on your ranch, wouldn't you?"

"I reckon I would."

"I learned a while back that as long as I'm with Tori, I can be happy anywhere."

The words stung unexpectedly. Lately, any future without Kit didn't appeal, even if the best-case scenario happened and he could keep JPX Ranch.

Had his fear of losing someone he loved made him miss out on something more important?

A wife and family?

He urged the horse into a trot. It wouldn't do any good to think about it now. He'd made his choices. He'd have to live with them.

"Have another doughnut."

Kit happily took one from the box Tori

held out. The two of them sat on the back deck, which lined the entire rear of the house. The view before them was breathtaking, with mountains, trees, a river snaking in the distance and meadows for miles.

"I always bring snacks on these adventures." Tori bit into a powdered sugar doughnut and dusted off the crumbs that fell on her shirt. "Junk food is essential for my sanity. Red is meticulous, which is code for *s-l-o-w*."

Kit chuckled. "How long have you been looking for land?"

"Two months. We originally were looking in Montana, but there's something about Wyoming."

"There is, isn't there?" Kit nibbled away at her doughnut and relaxed into the chair. "This is living."

"It is. I could see myself having coffee out here in the summer. Putting a Christmas tree up next to the big stone fireplace. Riding horseback around the property with

Red. Hanging out with the kids when they come to visit."

Kit had already explained to Tori about her and Wade's relationship, and Cam dying. Tori had told her about their kids—one married and one a senior in college—and how she and Red had missed farming and ranching for the past five years.

"That friend of yours, he single?"

"Yep." Kit hoped Tori wasn't thinking of setting him up with someone.

"You know, finding a partner in life is important. He seems to really like you."

"We've been friends a long time. He does like me. Just not the way you're implying."

She pursed her lips. "I saw the way he acted with you. Protective. Caring."

"Yeah, that's Wade." She had the strongest urge to stand up and pace. She resisted.

"Are you worried about raising the baby on your own? Sure is a shame your husband passed."

"I would have been raising the baby on my own even if he'd lived." She'd come to terms with it. In some ways, it had kept her from falling apart after Cam's heart attack. "My husband was adamant he wanted a divorce."

"Well, look at me putting my foot in my mouth…" She looked mortified.

"Don't feel bad. I stayed with him too long and for the wrong reasons. It took me until recently to understand that."

"Red drives me batty sometimes, but at the end of the day, he's my best friend."

Kit took another bite of the doughnut. Cam had never been her best friend.

Wade was. Always had been.

"Red's having a difficult time making a decision. He's not one for change."

"Change is hard." Kit finished the rest of the pastry. "I'm struggling with it right now myself."

"Once you're settled and holding that darling baby in your arms, it will all be worth it. You'll see."

"Is that how it was for you? With your kids?"

"Yes. I was surprised at how slow the baby

years went by, but the school years? Flew by faster than a tornado. And then the kids were gone. Off living their own lives. Made me appreciate Red even more."

Kit couldn't stand to think that far ahead. If the baby lived, he'd grow up and leave her.

She'd be all alone again.

"We've had our ups and downs. Debt years. Flush years. Sickness. Health. You name it. I wouldn't change a thing, though." Tori stared off into the distance with a gentle smile on her face.

Would Kit have changed a thing about her life? Before finding out she was pregnant, she would have probably said yes. But now? If she hadn't married Cam, or if he'd have left her sooner, she wouldn't have this precious child inside her.

The sounds of footsteps caught her attention. The screen door opened.

"Give us a few days to discuss it, and I'll get back to you," Red said as he shook Wade's hand.

"Well, I guess that's our cue," Kit said to

Tori while the men wrapped things up with Joe. "Thanks for keeping me company."

"I enjoyed talking to you, honey. Take care of that baby. And don't worry. It will all work out the way it's supposed to."

Kit wanted to believe it would, but the way life had been going didn't convince her. A few minutes later, she waved goodbye and walked with Wade out to his truck.

As he backed up and pulled away, Kit let her head fall against the headrest. "What nice people."

"They are. I was surprised to see them here. Ray usually tells me when there's a showing." Wade adjusted the air-conditioning with one hand while steering with the other. They passed fields as they drove to the main road.

"Do you think they'll buy it?" She watched an eagle soaring above.

"I'm not sure. He seemed enthusiastic, but he was adamant Tori had to approve."

"She seemed to like it."

"You think so?" He slowed when they

drove under the sign hanging from two log posts. Then he took a right and soon they were speeding west toward home. "I'm glad you came with me. Thank you." He reached over and squeezed her hand.

Her chest expanded. It felt really nice to be appreciated.

As he turned his attention back to the road, she studied his profile. He'd been patient, kind, considerate, selfless and all around wonderful to her since she'd arrived.

Tori had Red.

And Kit wanted Wade.

She loved him.

Simply loved him.

Possible snapshots from the future ran through her mind one by one. Of her and Wade rocking on the front porch. Holding their babies. Riding around the ranch. Church on Sundays with their friends.

None of those snapshots would ever be taken.

Because she and Wade weren't meant to be together.

The only way she'd ever get married again was if the relationship was built on love, commitment and a strong faith in God. Wade didn't love her, showed no signs of wanting commitment and she wasn't sure where his faith in God stood.

In less than a week, she'd be starting a new life, which meant she had to get over Wade Croft.

# Chapter Twelve

"We are wearing cowboy boots, right?" Wade asked Marshall at the men's store Thursday afternoon. They were having their final tuxedo fittings for the wedding on Saturday. He was faking a chipper mood for Marshall's sake. Yesterday, after leaving Dudley Farms, he'd wanted to tell Kit the truth about his finances, but she'd been quiet, and before long, asleep.

He hadn't had the heart to wake her up. And the moment passed, and here he was, wondering why keeping it from her was so important. Keeping it from the guys, on the other hand…

"You even have to ask?" Marshall looked disgusted.

"Well, what are these for, then?" Nash held up shiny black shoes.

Marshall hitched his thumb over his shoulder. "As far as I'm concerned, you can leave them here. I'm not wearing them."

"What is this color?" Clint held the bow tie up. His wife had planned Marshall and Ainsley's wedding. "Lexi was adamant it had to be ice blue, not periwinkle, not royal blue, not baby blue. Ice blue. I had to promise to give her the exact description or she was coming along."

Nash took it from him and squinted. "How can you tell what the difference is?"

Wade and Marshall crowded around them. They stared at the tie for several minutes.

"Just take a picture of it and send it to her." Wade slid his arms into the black tuxedo jacket. "It looks like the sky to me, but what do I know?"

"Ainsley will love it, no matter what it's called. Tell Lexi not to worry." Marshall checked out his reflection in one of the three-way mirrors. "What do you think?"

"Looking good, man." Wade clapped his hand on Marshall's shoulder.

Nash whistled. Clint nodded his approval.

When all four of them had their tuxes on, Wade handed the salesclerk his phone. "We need a picture of this. Who would have thought when we met as thirteen-year-olds we'd still be best friends all these years later?"

The clerk took several photos and returned the phone to Wade.

"Who would have thought we'd be living near Sweet Dreams?" Nash slipped the phone into his pocket. "Marsh, you need to move back as soon as Ainsley's done with nursing school."

"We might. We've talked about it." Marshall shot Wade a wicked grin. "Isn't it time you got on it, Wade?"

"Got on what?" He widened his stance. Lately, all he could think about was Kit and the baby and her leaving.

"Claiming your bride."

"We'll lasso you up and force you if necessary." Nash slung his arm over Wade's shoulders. Wade shrugged it off. Lasso him up. As if they could.

"Maybe he's not going to get married," Clint said.

That Clint, he was a good guy.

"And maybe he's too chicken." Nash high-fived Marshall.

"All right. Stop." Wade thrust his palms out. "It's not happening. Although I think it's safe to say I've been thinking things."

"Did you hear that?" Nash elbowed Clint. "He's thinking things."

Wade glowered at Nash, who, thankfully, shut up.

"I'm not as against marriage as I once was." He took off the jacket. "But I'm not in a situation to do anything about it. That's all I'm saying. Don't read too much into it."

"Is it Kit?" Clint asked. "She's mourning her husband, I guess. I hope Lexi would mourn me if I died."

"The marriage wasn't great at the end, so I couldn't say for sure." He wanted to change the subject, to go back to not being in the spotlight. "But I don't think she's pining for him, if that's what you're asking. She's determined to move to Casper. Soon."

"To be close to the hospital, right?" Nash grew serious. "Amy told me about the little guy's heart condition."

Wade nodded.

"Don't assume anything." Marshall undid the tie. "She might be in love with you and you don't know it."

"No one's talking about love." He gulped. Did Kit love him? And why did the thought fill him with so much hope? "I couldn't do anything about it if she did." But if Red made an offer on Dudley Farms... *God, have mercy. Please let me sell it.* Then, and only then, could he explore the feelings he was having about Kit. But all the money in the world couldn't guarantee forever. "What time is the rehearsal dinner again?"

"We're meeting at the church at six tomorrow night, then heading over to Belle and Raleigh's for the rehearsal dinner. Raleigh's having a pig roast."

While Nash jabbered on about how hungry he was, Clint just stared at Wade. Why was he looking at him like that?

When he could take the scrutiny no longer, Wade closed the distance between them. "What? You obviously have something on your mind."

Clint's jaw clenched, but he nodded. "You remember the night I came to your ranch? I'd just told Lexi I was quitting as her ranch manager. I didn't think we could be together."

"I remember." How could he forget it? He'd never seen Clint so distraught. And the next morning, when Clint had been transparent about his feelings, not only about Lexi but about his childhood, it had stuck with Wade.

Clint tilted his head to the side. "You're heading for a bad time if you don't acknowledge what's going on between you and Kit."

"There's nothing—"

"There's something."

Wade ground his teeth together. He could feel the pulse in his temple throb. He refused to say another word.

"Figure out what you want. Then go for it. You'll regret it if you don't."

Marshall and Nash hovered near them.

"You told me the same thing, Wade, six months ago," Marshall said. "It's time to follow your own advice."

"And you would have told me, too, but I was too thickheaded to confide in you guys." Nash grinned.

"I can't have her." His blood pressure was skyrocketing. Wouldn't they just let him be?

Clint exchanged glances with Nash and Marshall.

"I messed up. I bought Dudley Farms, and the crops went bust last year, the equipment is shot, I have no money for seed, I mortgaged my ranch to borrow the money for the property, and I'm up to my ears in bills that I'm dangerously close to not being able to pay."

He took a breath, surprised at how freeing it was to lay it all out there.

"I've been there, man." Clint nodded. "Desperate."

"So have I." Nash rubbed his chin.

"Me, too." Marshall stepped forward. "You need to pray about it."

Prayer. They were always harping on about prayer.

And this time it was such a relief.

"I agree," he said softly.

Three sets of raised eyebrows met him.

"I'm not saying everything's going to turn out all hunky-dory, but I've been talking to the good Lord again." A little, at least.

"Good. We want to see you happy."

"Who says I'm not happy?"

None of them seemed convinced.

"Fine, I'll pray and think about what I want. Now leave me alone."

"If you need money to get you through…" Each man made the offer. He turned each one down.

"I appreciate it. Appreciate you—every

one of you. I'll get through this. One of the properties will sell. In the meantime, I'm looking for a buyer for Del Poncho."

"I'll buy Del Poncho. You know I've always loved that horse." Nash seemed serious, not like he was making the offer out of pity.

"Whoa! Wait. You have JPX Ranch up for sale?" Clint asked.

"Yeah."

"But it's…everything to you."

Lately, it hadn't been feeling like everything. Lately, Kit had been feeling more important.

"Yeah, well, things change." He shrugged, trying not to think about losing his ranch.

Marshall rubbed his chin. "When I get back from the honeymoon, I'll come up to Dudley Farms and take a look at the faulty equipment. Maybe I can get it running. Won't help you much this summer, but it would be fixed for next year."

This was why he should have confided in them all sooner. Marshall repaired large machinery for a living. Why hadn't Wade asked him for help last spring when it could have made a difference? No sense kicking himself. He would make better choices from now on.

"I appreciate it, Marshall. And it might not be necessary if the place sells. Concentrate on the wedding. I hope you're packing plenty of sunscreen for the beach."

They all took the hint and started talking about Marshall's honeymoon destination.

Not long after, they split up in the parking lot, saying that they'd see each other the next day for the rehearsal.

Instead of driving home, Wade drove out to the shack. He took long strides to the front door. After unlocking it, he poked around the rooms. Still had mice droppings. Same small rooms and a few pieces of dusty furniture.

Memories of poring over property listings at the tiny table crashed over him. He'd been so sure of himself and his future back then. Nothing would have stopped him, and nothing had. Here he was, years later, and he'd had success.

But whether he lived on JPX Ranch, Dudley Farms or here in the shack, he had no one to share his life with.

Pulling out one of the kitchen chairs, he dusted off the seat and collapsed onto it.

He wanted Kit and the baby. By his side.

But what did he have to give her?

If an offer from Red came in, he'd have money. Land. His name. Security.

It would be enough for most women. However, Kit wasn't most women.

And what if Red didn't make the offer? Wade couldn't bear to say goodbye to her and let her move in to the apartment. He wanted to feel the baby kick and help her get to her appointments and hold her hand when she needed it.

He wanted her in his life. All the time. Not just on a come-and-go basis.

But naming this feeling wasn't happening. Because the *L* word made you vulnerable, and sometimes the people you loved disappeared suddenly, leaving you alone and broken.

He'd been alone and broken for a long time.

If he offered Kit protection and a home, but not the emotional part, would it be enough to convince her to take a chance on him?

She double-checked the order for new bedding and towels before finalizing the online purchase. A 70 percent off clearance had proved fruitful. Plans swirled in her mind. She should be happy. She'd have plenty of time to settle into her new home before the appointments with the obstetrician and the cardiologist.

The baby moved, and she smiled at her belly. He was growing stronger every day.

It didn't mean the hole in his heart had gone away, though. He wasn't in the clear. But she'd be the first to admit she'd let down her guard ever since learning he didn't have special needs. Maybe she'd been wrong to enjoy this time. Should she be worrying? He could still die.

She wouldn't think about it.

Life progressed on a day-by-day basis right now. No more long-term planning until after the baby was born. She'd get a plan together then.

She padded to the window. This had been a peaceful interlude. She hated to leave it. She'd miss the ranch, this airy, wonderful cabin and, most of all, Wade.

The box of baby supplies Sandra had sent her stood in the corner. A purple envelope with the greeting card peeked out. She'd forgotten she'd been waiting to open it. But now there was nothing holding her back. Sliding the card out, she studied the front, an illustrated elephant mama with a baby. Very cute.

A note fell out, fluttering to the floor. Carefully, she bent to pick it up. Then she smoothed it open.

Dear Kit,
I hope this card finds you and the baby well. You've been heavy on my heart

and in my prayers. It seems so cruel for you to lose your husband at the same time you're having a baby. I can't pretend to know what you're going through, but I understand loss. I had two miscarriages and a stillborn child before the Lord blessed us with Greta and Mark. The only thing that got me through—and continues to get me through—is knowing I will see each of my babies in heaven. God is taking care of them for me, just like He's taking care of Cam. Hold on to your faith. In the end, it's all that matters.

Your friend,

Sandra

The card had almost a dozen signatures, all teachers she used to work with. Blurry-eyed, she sat on the edge of the bed. Cam had been a Christian. A sinner, too, but who wasn't?

God was taking care of Cam.

A wave of emotion hit her. Did she want

God taking care of him? *Lord, I'm tired of holding on to this anger and guilt. Forgive me for losing control the night he died, and forgive Cam for causing me so much pain.*

She couldn't get over that Sandra had lost three babies. An ache stole up her torso. How had her friend been able to go on after those losses? And to maintain her faith—it blew Kit away.

Sandra had lost children and kept trying to have them. That was brave.

Could Kit describe herself that way?

Was it brave to be in love with Wade and not tell him? Was she taking the easy way out by moving next week?

What did she really want?

She wanted a life side by side with Wade, kids, friends, Sweet Dreams, all of it.

It was probably an unrealistic fantasy. Even if she got it, it would fall apart somehow. She'd try to make him happy, but he'd get tired of evenings rocking on the porch.

She wouldn't be enough for him.

She wrung her hands together.

Were those a bunch of lies? Shouldn't she at least take a chance on having the future she wanted?

She wasn't brave. The thought of telling Wade the truth about how she felt made her want to vomit.

Heat flushed over her skin. The stress must be getting to her.

Wade's knee bounced in double time at supper that night. He wasn't used to feeling so out of sorts. And was he imagining it, or did Kit look pale?

Red and Tori wanted to tour JPX Ranch tomorrow bright and early. He knew they were going to love it. It would solve all his problems, but it was a loss he couldn't bear to contemplate. Moving from his home? Imagining the look on Jackson's face if he could see what Wade had done? His appetite vanished.

He might as well get it over with and tell Kit the truth about his money problems. Tomorrow morning she'd wonder why Tori and Red were here.

He hated admitting he'd failed. Hated it.

"Do you have plans tomorrow for lunch?" he asked. The words he should be saying wouldn't form.

"Not really."

"Want to go back to the river for another picnic?" *Tell her, already!*

Her smile lit her face. "I'd love to."

He couldn't look away from her green eyes. They were tinted with concerns. He could guess what they were. Would the baby be okay? Would she do all right in a new town on her own? Other worries were in there, too, but he couldn't decipher them.

"I've got to be back by five to get ready for the rehearsal. I'd still like for you to come with me if you're up for it."

"Okay." She averted her eyes. "I'll see how I feel."

He lunged for his glass of water again and, in his haste, spilled a few drops. Meals and conversations had never been this uncomfortable in the past. Why couldn't he tell her what was on his mind?

They ate in silence for a while. He managed to choke down a few bites.

"Wade?"

"Yeah?"

"I'm feeling more peace about Cam lately."

Cam? The last person Wade wanted to discuss. His blood still boiled when he thought about how the guy had cheated on her.

She continued. "For a while I had all these regrets, like I should have left him after the first time he cheated. But I can see now I would have lost other things if I'd left."

"You mean the baby?" He leaned back in his chair.

"Yes." She sighed. "You told me I wasn't responsible for Cam's death, and I really didn't believe you."

"You weren't. You yelled at him. People yell at each other every day, and they don't die."

"I know. But I hated him. When he told me he wanted to marry the other woman, I hated them both. My head knows I didn't kill him, but my heart wasn't getting the memo until recently."

"Kit…" He lowered his voice. "Let it go. You never could have anticipated he would die of a heart attack."

He couldn't see her face, but she had an air of defeat about her.

Crossing over to her, he pulled her out of the chair and into his arms.

"Don't do this to yourself. You're the kindest person I know. You would never knowingly hurt anyone."

"I hurt people. I do it all the time." She looked up at him. "I repent, and the next thing I know, I've sinned again."

"We all do. We don't even mean to."

"I prayed about it. I forgave him. And I asked God to forgive me, too."

He held her for a few minutes. "While we're being real, I have something to tell you."

Questions lurked in her eyes.

"I had to put the ranch up for sale."

She wrenched free from his grasp. "Why?"

"I messed up." He stepped to the patio door and eyed the outbuildings in the distance. Then he faced her again. "I couldn't afford Dudley Farms." He explained how he'd taken the loans out, and the series of disasters that had dried up his assets. "Red and Tori are coming out here tomorrow, and maybe God will have mercy on me and they'll buy it."

"Oh, Wade, but then you'd lose it. I know how much you love this ranch."

He clenched his jaw, nodding curtly. "It's better than losing everything. I have to accept the consequences of my poor choice."

"I'm sorry." She sidled up next to him, wound her arms around his waist and laid her head against his chest.

"I am, too. But it will work out." He had to believe it would.

"Wade, you've helped me come to terms with my guilt. I'm returning the favor. You made a business decision, and it didn't work out the way you'd hoped. I don't want you to feel bad. Taking a chance isn't a sin."

He had to take responsibility for this. "You're right, but the reason for me taking the chance *was* a sin. I got greedy. Thought I was invincible. I think I assumed everything I touched would succeed."

He held his breath, searching her eyes for disgust or disappointment.

"Repent and move on. God is our good Father. He loves us and comforts us when we make mistakes. I'm still getting used to the concept." She stepped back, shivering. "Do you mind if I skip the rest of dinner? My nerves must be getting to me. I feel tired."

"No problem. I'll take you over right now."

He helped her into the truck and drove her to the cabin. Part of him hoped she'd change her mind and invite him to sit on the porch with her like she usually did, but she slipped into the cabin with a tiny wave and that was that.

He drove back to the house.

It felt empty.

Lonely.

He'd never felt all that lonely before, so what had changed?

Kit. She'd changed him. And he couldn't go back to the way things were.

He didn't really want to go back to that life. He didn't want to eat alone, or miss feeling the baby kick. Didn't want to be deprived of Kit's conversation, her smile, her easy ways.

He headed straight to his bedroom, threw himself on the king-size bed and turned on a baseball game.

She hadn't judged him for his financial predicament. And she'd made it sound as if all he had to do was repent and he could move forward guilt-free. Her claiming God was a Father who loved and comforted him sounded good. Who wouldn't want some of that? But he'd never had a father. Big Bob at Yearling was the closest thing he'd had, and then Jackson had taken him under his wing.

*God, I'm sorry for taking my blessings for*

*granted. For letting my greed get the best of me.*

Kit was the best person he knew. Why did bad things happen to good people? *Lord, heal Kit's baby. Let him grow up to be a strong, fine man.*

Wade's mom hadn't deserved to be kidnapped and killed. If she'd lived, his life would have turned out differently. He might not have felt the need to protect his heart so thoroughly.

What did it matter? She *had* been kidnapped and murdered. He'd grown up an orphan. Kit had, too.

He understood how life worked. Could accept that it wasn't fair.

He wanted it to be fair for Kit, though. He'd do about anything to make life fair for her.

# Chapter Thirteen

"Best news I've heard in months. Thanks, Ray." Wade had been waiting for news for the past two hours. Red and Tori had toured JPX Ranch all morning with Wade by their side, and he'd been certain they loved it. But they'd shocked him when they'd exchanged glances and told him the ranch was nice but not for them. His heart had sunk like a boulder to the bottom of a lake. Their next words had blown him away. They told him to expect an offer on Dudley Farms within a few hours.

He'd almost collapsed, but he'd willed himself to stay standing as he thanked them, pumped their hands and mentally praised the Lord.

Now here he was, sitting next to Kit after the picnic, his cell phone in hand as Ray confirmed it. Red and Tori were offering him just below asking price for Dudley Farms. His financial crisis would be officially over as soon as the deal closed.

"You're not going to believe this." Wade turned to Kit, who was relaxing on the quilt. A slight breeze teased her hair as she rested on her elbows with her face tipped up to the sky. She looked pale, but content.

"What?"

"I sold Dudley Farms!"

She shot to a seated position, her eyes wide with excitement. "You did? Red and Tori?"

"Yep." He got to his feet and pumped his fist in the air. "Yes!"

She slowly stood up, laughing. And all the thoughts and things he'd been feeling collided into this moment.

He'd sold the land.

He could support Kit and the baby. He finally had something to offer her. And he wasn't going to let the moment slip away.

"Let's watch the water from there." He hitched his head toward the wooden bridge crossing the river. He held his hand out. When she took it, her soft skin and warm touch calmed his nerves. He was doing the right thing.

As they strolled toward the bridge Kit pointed out a pair of small yellow birds darting from tree to tree. She always saw the beauty in nature. He liked that about her.

When they reached the middle of the bridge, they both leaned on the rail.

"It looks shallow," she said. "Does the water usually recede so quickly?"

"Yes. It will be more of a creek by August. Your ankles will get wet and that's about it."

He watched her for a moment as he considered his next words.

"What's going on?" She shifted to face him.

He wasn't surprised. She'd always been able to read him.

He hadn't planned this out enough. What should he do? What should he say?

She stared at him expectantly and the moment stretched to uncomfortable proportions. Finally, he took her hands in his.

"I don't want you to go."

"I know you don't." She looked to the side.

"I want you to stay. Forever."

She jerked, her face all screwed up. "What?"

"I think we should get married."

She blinked. Twice. "Why?"

*Why?* He racked his brain. *Oh, right.*

"Now that I've sold Dudley Farms, I'll be able to pay off the loans, and I'll have cash left over in the bank. Plenty of it. You won't have to worry about money ever again. I'll give you and the baby my name. I promise I will be faithful. I will be the best husband I can be to you, and I'll be the best father to your son, too."

Her cheeks were flushed. Her eyes darted back and forth.

"Sweet Dreams is perfect for you," he

said. "My friends think you're great, and I know you like them. We can make a life together here."

She took a step backward, slipping her hands from his. She looked small, young, fragile—and so much like the girl he'd met all those years ago, it took his breath away.

"You're offering me everything I've ever wanted."

Hope surged through his chest.

"What about love?" she asked quietly.

He couldn't breathe. His lips refused to form the words she wanted to hear.

"You know I care about you." He prayed it would be enough.

"I see. Yes, I know you care about me. But everything you offered? Isn't very much in the end." She met his gaze and held it.

What was she getting at? He massaged his neck absentmindedly.

She placed her hand on his arm. "Thank you, Wade. You're the most generous man I know. I'm floored you care enough to propose. I'd be a fool to turn you down."

He held his breath, waiting for her answer. Hoping…hoping…

"But I love you too much to accept. I'd rather live in poverty with a man who loves me than live in a mansion with a man who doesn't."

She loved him? His heart stopped beating. It was as if someone had dropped him in the ocean and he was floundering, desperately trying to latch on to a life raft. And he was right back to being a scared little kid moving in to his first foster home. He didn't trust love. It hadn't been enough to keep him and his mom together. She'd loved him, too.

She continued. "You're the best friend I've ever had. I want to keep it that way. If I accepted your proposal, I'd resent the fact you don't love me the way I love you. And you would resent me, too."

"I would never resent you."

"You would." Tears swam in her eyes, and her wide smile held so much tenderness. "I can't believe I'm turning you down. You just offered me everything I ever wanted. The perfect family, a ranch, wide-open spaces, financial security, friends. A place to set roots."

"Then say yes." He grabbed her hand and pressed closer to her.

"I want more. I don't want to be your roommate."

He sucked in a breath. More? How much more could he give?

"I had a loveless marriage once." Her voice cracked. "I won't have one again."

"It's not like that." He wanted to explain, to tell her their friendship was deep. They could build a life together. Blood rushed through his veins like the water rushing over the rocks upstream. "It wouldn't be like that."

She gave him a wan smile. "I think we should go back. I'm skipping the rehearsal and dinner. It's for the best."

Why couldn't he say the words she needed to hear? Love was the one thing he couldn't give.

"Fine." He marched ahead, grabbing the picnic supplies and the quilt. They strode in silence back to his truck. He pressed the gas pedal a little too forcefully as he drove away.

Shame crushed his shoulders.

He'd offered her everything. He had nothing else to give. His heart had been out of order since his mother disappeared.

Of all the decisions she'd made in her life, this one had been both the easiest and the hardest. It went against all logic. Her limbs were frozen as Wade opened the door to help her out of the truck. As soon as his hand was on her arm, she sprang into action. She tripped a little on the way to the ground, but he held her steady.

She'd just turned down those strong arms forever.

He tempted her to take it all back. To cling to him, begging for him to ask her again, and, yes, this time she'd agree to marry him, whether he loved her or not.

She wanted to be Mrs. Wade Croft so badly her knees almost buckled.

"I can take it from here." Her voice

sounded tight and crackly even to her ears. It couldn't be helped. Only a dozen feet separated her from temptation and common sense.

*Please don't say anything.* She turned to the cabin. Then disappointment set in as she realized he had no words, anyway. The silence prodded her forward. As soon as she slipped inside, the sound of the truck driving away met her ears. She closed the door, squeezed her eyes shut and stood with her back to it.

Had she just made the worst mistake of her life?

She'd never in a million years guessed he would offer to marry her.

It was so typical of Wade, she was kind of surprised she hadn't anticipated it. He'd always stepped up for her in ways no one else ever did. And he'd stepped up big-time. He'd offered her so much…

She lurched forward, wobbling slightly. The day had been too much. She couldn't make sense of it. Taking it slow, she headed to the bedroom. Had she really said no to his proposal?

He would be faithful. She had no doubt. He was a man of his word and always had been.

His kisses came to mind, along with all the ooey-gooey feelings. She would never forget his hard chest against hers, his powerful arms around her or the tenderness of his lips.

Wouldn't it be worth the disappointment of him not loving her just to have a lifetime of those kisses?

She climbed on top of the bed and stared at the ceiling.

No, it wouldn't. Because every time she'd sit down to dinner, she'd be hoping he'd give her and the baby his entire attention. Every time he came in after a long day, she would want him to wrap her in his arms and kiss her soundly because he loved her and missed her, not because he felt obligated.

Without love, she'd never be the most important part of his life.

But he was already the most important part of hers.

Her heart sliced open. Why hadn't she protected herself the way she'd told herself she would? She should have taken the disgusting hotel room weeks ago and never come back here.

She turned on her side with her hands on her belly. The baby was all that mattered. Her focus had drifted to selfish wants. If her heart was breaking, it was her own fault.

*God, I did the right thing, didn't I?*

All she could see was Cam's face when she'd shown him the pregnancy test. His eyes had filled with equal parts panic and loathing.

He'd loathed her.

She'd tried to forget the final words he'd said to her after their terrible fight. They rang as clear and hateful as the day he'd said them. *I never loved you. I pitied you.* And he'd slammed out the door. It had been the last time she saw him alive.

He'd never loved her.

He'd taken pity on her.

And Wade was doing the same thing.

She'd been right to turn Wade down. A pity proposal would end the same way her marriage with Cam had—with bitter regrets, hateful words and not an ounce of friendship left.

Mindlessly, she rubbed her stomach.

Then she sat up.

She hadn't felt the baby in hours. How long had it been? She thought back to when she'd last felt him move. This morning? Breakfast, maybe.

She tried not to panic, but worst-case scenarios popped up over and over in her mind. With shaking fingers, she found the number of the obstetrician in town. She dialed it, pressed through the menu options and was put on hold.

She'd lost her husband and career in Fort Laramie.

She'd lost her shot at her dream life with Wade.

She couldn't lose her baby, too.

\* \* \*

"You haven't said more than three words all night, and you look like ten miles of dirt road." Nash set a plate towering with food on the table next to Wade.

Wade glared at him.

Marshall's sister, Belle, had insisted on hosting the rehearsal dinner. The pole barn had been cleaned up and decorated for the event, and at least thirty people milled about. Laughter filled the air. Marshall and Ainsley were standing arm in arm near a group of people in the corner. Their love was so obvious, it almost nauseated him.

That could have been him and Kit.

But he'd blown it.

"What happened?" Nash leaned back, turning to face Wade.

"I sold Dudley Farms."

"That's great news!" He held his hand up for a high five and dropped it when Wade ignored him. "Isn't it?"

"Yep."

"So what's the problem?"

He wasn't having this conversation. He was eating the food, then walking over to the blissful couple and saying goodbye. It was high time he licked his wounds and slunk away like the injured animal he was.

"You might as well fess up." Nash cracked his knuckles. "I'll get it out of you one way or another."

"Leave me alone." He hunched over the plate. His appetite had fled town long ago. Why was he even still here?

"Not until you tell me what has you so worked up."

"What's going on over here?" Clint dropped into the seat next to Wade.

"Someone's having a bad day." Nash arched his eyebrows and pointed to Wade.

"Will you mind your own business?" He should ignore them.

"He sold Dudley Farms. Doesn't look too happy about it."

"You do look...defeated." Clint's low, quiet voice was the final straw.

"Well, maybe I am." He shoved the plate

to the side. "I asked Kit to marry me, and she said no. There. Are you happy now?"

Nash and Clint exchanged wide-eyed glances. Wade wanted to wipe his hands down his face, but he wouldn't give them the satisfaction.

"Why'd she say no?" Clint asked.

He balled his hands into fists and rested them on the table. He clenched and un-clenched his jaw. Couldn't these two take the hint?

"Maybe she's shy about getting married again." Nash snapped his fingers.

"She's not shy about marriage." Wade hadn't meant to say anything, but there it was.

"Okay, well, maybe she's not ready. She's got so much on her mind with the baby and all…" Nash scratched the back of his neck. "Those pregnancy hormones are nothing to mess with. Trust me, I know. Every other minute Amy's in tears over something. I don't know what to do. I just hand her an ice cream bar. Sometimes she's grateful, but last night she snapped at me. And then she started crying again…"

"It's not pregnancy hormones," he said through gritted teeth.

"I really thought she liked you." Clint rubbed his chin.

"She does like me." Was he having an allergic reaction to something? His throat felt as if it was swelling up.

"Maybe she's not attracted to you. It happens." Nash shrugged.

He vividly remembered her response when he'd kissed her. "That's not it."

"You sound awfully sure about that." Nash raised an eyebrow.

Wade ignored him.

"Do you know why she turned you down?" Clint asked.

*Yes.*

"What kind of question is that, Clint?" Nash shook his head. "Like kicking a man while he's down."

As if Nash wasn't doing the same thing. At Clint's crestfallen face, Wade sighed. These were his friends. His best friends. They knew everything about him. He could trust them with this, too.

"I offered her and the baby my name, the ranch, financial security, a lifelong commitment."

Nash and Clint nodded.

"But she wanted love."

Both edged back in their chairs with straight spines.

"And you didn't tell her you loved her?" Nash asked.

Wade shook his head.

"Can't say I blame her," Clint said.

Nash let out a disgusted sigh. "And why didn't you? We all know you love her. It's as plain as the sun rising each morning."

He did love her.

He loved her.

Not as a brother or a friend.

He loved her the way a man loved a woman.

Why hadn't he been able to admit it?

*God, I'm scared. Loving means losing, doesn't it?*

"You're right. I love her. I couldn't admit it, not even to myself." He dropped his forehead into his hands. He couldn't remember the last time he'd cried. Probably the night he'd been separated from Kit as a kid. But emotions pounded in his chest.

His friends probably thought he was a weak fool. He couldn't bear to look at either of them.

"I've been there, brother." Nash put his hand on Wade's shoulder.

"Me, too." Clint nodded, his eyes full of concern.

Wade took a drink of water to try to loosen the knot in his throat.

"The question you should be asking is what are you going to do about it?" Nash asked.

"I don't know." Here came the part where they told him to rush back home and tell her in no uncertain terms he loved her.

He wasn't up for it.

Clint shifted in his seat. "You didn't pray about the situation, did you?"

No, he hadn't. He'd prayed. Just not about his relationship with Kit.

"It wasn't until I got right with the Lord that I could find my way forward with Amy," Nash said.

"Same here with Lexi." Clint nodded.

"Hasn't it sunk in yet? You're not in control of your life." Clint crossed his arms over his chest.

"Try not to take this the wrong way, man, but things have always come kind of easy to you," Nash said. "You might not have felt like you needed to pray. This isn't one of those times. Get on those knees. Find out God's will."

"How in the world am I supposed to know God's will?" He threw his hands up in the air. "It's not like He's coming down and speaking to me. There's no burning bush on my ranch. I can pray and pray and pray, but how do I really know I've got the answer?"

"The Bible." Clint rapped his knuckles on the table.

"It is the living Word." Nash lifted one

shoulder. "You've got to at least try. Pray. Read the Bible. The Holy Spirit will guide you if you ask Him."

"Since when did you become the expert?"

"I've been going to Bible class with Amy." His face reddened. "I'm no expert, though."

"If I tell you I'll pray about it, will you get off my back?" He glared at Nash, then Clint.

Clint held his palms at his chest. "I can't force you to depend on God. Pray or don't. It's your decision."

"But *I* think you should," Nash said.

Wade thought he should, too.

"I'm out of here. I'll see you at the wedding tomorrow." Tipping his hat to them, he stood. After finding Marshall and Ainsley and wishing them well for the night, he strode out to his truck. The sun had dropped low in the sky, leaving streaks of pastel colors.

As he began the drive home, he flicked off the radio and let his thoughts adjust to the silence.

*God, I messed up.*

He didn't know what to say. It wasn't as if God didn't know all his thoughts, anyhow.

Kit's face earlier, as she'd told him she loved him on the bridge, kept intruding in his mind.

*I should have told her the truth. I love her. What do I do now?*

The only answer was the sound of the air-conditioning blowing.

Maybe the Bible would have the answers he was looking for. When he got home, he'd dust off the good book and attempt to find out.

He had to do something.

He just hoped it wasn't too late.

# Chapter Fourteen

Kit jolted awake. Her skin burned. Why was she so hot? She tried to kick off the covers, but her legs refused to move. The covers weighed a thousand pounds. The clock showed 3:03 a.m. Where was she? The dim room came into view. She was still in the cabin on Wade's ranch. A searing pain in her back made her teeth clench. She forced her legs over the side of the bed, braced her hand under her stomach and hobbled toward the bathroom.

Oh, no, she was going to throw up.

A wave of dizziness stopped the nausea. She groped for something to hold on to, and her hand found the bathroom door handle. Almost there.

Inside, she flicked on the light. A sheen of sweat covered her face. The pain in her back clenched again. She doubled over. What was wrong with her?

*Oh, God, not the baby!*

Although earlier she'd tried for over an hour, she hadn't gotten through to the doctor's office, and she'd been so tired, she must have fallen asleep. She had to get help. Wade would know what to do.

Her head was spinning. She couldn't straighten. Why wouldn't her feet move?

On her hands and knees, she crawled back to the bedroom to find her phone. The nightstand was a hundred miles away, but she crept to it. Finally, she reached up and grasped the phone.

The exertion made her temperature soar. Her arms no longer supported her, and she fell facedown on the fluffy rug. As she flitted near the edge of consciousness, she forced herself to focus. Somehow, she found Wade's contact and pressed it.

*God, I know You're here. Don't let the baby die. Get Wade here now. Please, Lord, save the baby!*

Pain drilled through her lower back on the first ring.

"Yeah?" He sounded curt and groggy.

"Help," she whispered. The phone fell out of her hand, and she lay on her side, unable to move.

Nausea threatened once again. She closed her eyes.

"Kit? Is that you? What's wrong?"

She opened her mouth to speak, but no words came out.

Nothing mattered anymore.

Nothing but the baby.

Wade shoved his feet into cowboy boots and sprinted to his truck. He needed to get to Kit. Fast. His truck spit gravel as he tore up the lane to the cabin.

*Help.* One word. Whispered in desperation.

Fear choked the blood out of his heart.

He couldn't lose her.

He. Could. Not. Lose. Her.

He slammed on the brakes in front of the cabin, unlocked the front door and raced inside. No sign of her in the living area. He looked into her bedroom and almost fell to his knees at the sight of her lying on her side on the rug. Her cheek rested on her arm.

Was she breathing?

He knelt beside her to check her pulse. Her skin was on fire. Quickly, he scooped her into his arms and marched straight out to the truck. He eased the seat back and strapped the seat belt around her. As much as he'd like to call 911 and have medical professionals take over, it wasn't an option. It would take too long for an ambulance to come.

Should he grab her purse? She'd need her insurance card and license. He ran in and spotted it on the table. Five seconds later, he was at the wheel and driving as fast as safely possible. When he reached the road, he looked right, then left. Sweet Dreams didn't have a hospital. He'd have to drive farther, to the nearest city.

Flooring the accelerator, he sped down the road, fear squeezing him from every direction. What would cause her to have a blazing fever and pass out?

Whatever it was, it wasn't good.

Kit was his best friend. The person who mattered most to him.

She couldn't lose the baby. It would destroy her.

*Take it all, Lord. Take the ranch, the land, the money—all of it—but let Kit and her baby live.*

She was the most precious thing in his life.

She'd always been the most precious thing in his life.

His eyes blurred as he thought back on all the times they'd spent together. The letters she'd sent him every week at Yearling. The late-night calls just because. The visits he'd made to her when she was in college. Their easy laughter and quiet comfort simply being with each other.

And other less fond memories came back, like when she'd told him she was engaged. Or her wedding day—she'd looked so beautiful. He'd about lost it when she'd said *"I do"* to another man. But he'd wanted her to be happy. It had been hard—no, torture—to pull back on their friendship to let her marriage get off the ground. Then Cam died. And Wade hadn't known how to react to his death.

She'd shown up on his porch as a widow with a baby on the way, and it had scared the snot out of him. Filled him with hope, too. Hope that he'd finally have a chance with her, the woman he'd loved for as long as he could remember. He'd been stupid to think he could protect himself by not telling her he loved her. This pain seared as much, if not more, than the pain of losing his mother.

"I love you, Kit." He reached over and pressed the back of his hand to her cheek. Still way too hot. The fever was soaring, and the fact she was barely conscious took him to bad mental places.

Was she going to die?

*Keep it together. Focus on the road. She needs you now.*

He slammed the heel of his hand into the steering wheel. He hated not having control.

Once more he was a little boy at the babysitter's, waiting for his mother to come get him. *She's just running late, sugar. Nothing to worry about.*

And the next days had passed in a blur until one day he'd woken up in a foster home. The first of many. And yet he'd clung to the hope his mom would come back for him.

Later, when he'd found out she'd been murdered, he'd shut down. Realizing the finality of it—she would never come get him—set the course for the rest of his life.

He'd put up protective barriers that hadn't protected him at all. He'd convinced himself he could control getting hurt or not by avoiding love. But love couldn't be any more dangerous than whatever was happening right now. He wasn't even married to Kit and the thought of losing her was ripping out his heart.

He'd rather love her and lose her than never have the chance.

The miles fell away and his tension rose higher and higher. He could see things clearly, things he'd never realized were cloudy before.

In all his business deals, he'd been missing out on the one thing that truly would make him happy, would give his life some meaning.

Last night he'd offered Kit a future.

A shabby future.

His throat felt raw. She'd been right to turn him down. She deserved better, more, the world.

If he could do it over, he would bare his soul, tell her the truth—that he needed her more than anything.

The miles sped by and the edge of the city came into view.

"We're almost there, Kitty Cat." He got choked up and had to grind his teeth for a moment before speaking again. "Hang tight."

*I can't lose her!*

He glanced at her round tummy.

*I can't lose the baby, either.*

He loved the child like it was his own.

Why was this happening? What if she died? What if she never knew how much he loved her?

He parked the truck and carried her to the emergency room, where the staff whisked her away while a receptionist handed him a clipboard. When he'd filled out the paperwork to the best of his knowledge, he found a seat in the waiting area and slumped in the chair.

All he could do now was pray.

Kit's eyelashes fluttered. Beeps and lights bombarded her. She moaned. Something was on her arm. Tubes. Why? A gentle touch on her hand made her turn her head.

"Try and stay still, hon." A woman in scrubs adjusted the IV in her arm.

Why was there an IV in her arm? She couldn't remember… She must be in the hospital. What had happened? What day was it? Why—

The baby.

Her hands flew to her stomach.

Still round.

Still there.

"The baby…" Her throat was dry.

"Shh…don't use up your energy."

She'd use up every ounce of her energy to find out if her baby was okay. "Is he alright?"

The nurse's forehead furrowed, and she called over her shoulder for someone to come in. "You still have a high fever," she told Kit. "We're trying to get it down. Try and stay calm."

Why wouldn't they tell her if the baby was okay?

What was happening?

She was losing him, wasn't she? What had she done wrong? Her breaths came in shallow gasps. Hopelessness left a vacuum in her heart. The letter Sandra had written swam through her mind. She'd lost babies.

*God is taking care of them. Hold on to your faith. In the end, it's all that matters.*

Kit didn't want God to take care of the baby for her. She wanted to raise him herself!

Two other people in scrubs entered and talked with the nurse in hushed voices. She couldn't make out what they were saying.

Where was Wade? He'd make it all better. He'd explain to her what was going on. He'd get them to talk to her. Slightly lifting her head, she tried to see across the room, but the nurse pressed her back. She felt funny, like her limbs were made of taffy.

Wade wasn't in here. And why would he be? She remembered his proposal, remembered turning him down. He must have driven her here, though.

He'd always stepped up and done his duty where she was concerned. Was that why he'd asked her to marry him? Was she his duty?

"Don't move. We need you to stay as still as possible for the baby's sake."

For the baby's sake… It meant her son was still alive, right?

"Is he—"

"Just relax." The nurse patted her hand while someone fiddled with the IV. "The doctor is coming soon. Rest."

Rest? She didn't want to rest. She wanted them to save her baby.

Her eyelids felt so heavy. She'd close them for a moment. Just a moment. The seconds before she'd called Wade earlier bombarded her. She'd been in bed. Hot, so hot. Crawling to the bathroom. The cramps…

"Save my baby." The words came out scratchy. Had she even said them? Or was she in a dream?

"I'll get you some ice chips," the nurse said. "They'll make you feel better."

Kit reached for her, wanting her to wait, to stay and answer her questions, but her hand grabbed air. Too late.

The story of her life.

Too late.

Always just a little too late.

Too late to save her marriage. Too late to save Cam.

Too late to beg Wade to hold her and never let her go.

He'd offered her everything she'd ever wanted. His name, his home, his protection, his money. Safety. Belonging.

Security.

And like the idiot she was, she'd turned it all down. If she could go back... *Yes. Say yes, Kit.*

She stopped fighting the grogginess. Maybe if she slept, she'd dream about Wade, and this time she'd accept his proposal. This time she'd say yes to what she'd always wanted.

But even in her half-awake state, she knew it was a fantasy. Saying yes wouldn't change reality.

She loved Wade. And he didn't love her back.

Her love wasn't enough for him.

Some things never changed.

\* \* \*

Wade jerked awake. Was Kit okay? His neck had a crick from him slumping in the waiting room chair. Sunlight brightened the area. He checked his watch. After eight thirty. He must have drifted off.

He rubbed his neck and crossed to the reception desk.

"Any word on Kit McAllistor?" He took in the other people sitting nearby. Most of them had the same bleary-eyed fear he couldn't shake. It had been hours since the staff whisked Kit away. Surely they knew something by now?

"I'm sorry, sir. I'm not authorized to say." Her compassionate eyes darted back to the computer screen.

He had a bad feeling about this. "I'm getting a coffee and will be right back. You'll let me know when I can see her?"

"Of course." Her sympathetic smile didn't put him at ease. "The cafeteria is down the hall. Vending machines are in the opposite direction."

He could barely lift his boots as he made his way to the cafeteria. Doctors and nurses passed by in their scrubs and lab coats. Beeps and muted conversations filtered to the hall from the rooms he passed. A double door up ahead swung open, revealing the cafeteria. He poured a large black coffee, paid for it and returned to the waiting area.

For all his talk with Clint and Nash about seeking God's will and praying, he had yet to open his Bible and actually do it. Wade set the coffee on an end table, dropped into a chair and pulled out his phone.

Fear roped around his heart for Kit. For the baby. But he scrolled through until finding a Bible app.

*Okay, God, now what?*

The app opened to a Bible verse. It was from John. He skimmed through it. Then read it again. *"In the world ye shall have tribulation."* Great.

But God overcame the world.

He frowned, trying to decipher what it meant in this situation.

He moved on to the Psalm Dottie used to read to them at night when he lived at Yearling. *"The Lord is my shepherd..."*

The valley of the shadow of death— yep. That described this situation. He read it again, carefully, pausing to grasp each phrase.

He sat back in the chair, mindlessly reached for the coffee and took a drink. Still hot.

*I've been so stupid, thinking I was so smart.*

Clint and Nash were right. He'd never been in control. He thought about all the years he'd avoided church and ignored God.

*I'm sorry, Lord. I didn't thank You or appreciate all You've blessed me with. I was arrogant. Thought I'd done it all myself. Didn't give You credit at all.*

Hanging his head, Wade felt the full weight of his sin claw through his body.

*Forgive me, Lord. Forgive me.*

He wiped his face with his hands, surprised at the emotions coming to the surface. Jesus had died for him. Out of love. The ultimate love. The ultimate sacrifice.

*God, I'd do the same for Kit. Please let
her live. Please! Save her. Save the baby.
I'm begging You.*

He couldn't bear to live in a world without her in it. She'd been his rock, his stabil-
ity, the anchor in his life for so many years.
He couldn't stand the thought of not seeing
her cute freckles, not listening to her tinkly
laugh, not rocking in chairs on the porch as
they appreciated the beauty of Wyoming.

The world would be a bleak, dark place
without her in it.

He thought of Jackson leaving him his entire estate. All because the old man had no
wife, no family, no kids.

Wade didn't want to end up the same. He
wanted to create a legacy. With Kit beside
him.

Peace spread from his heart to his mind.

*I've finally made it, Kit.* Choked up, he
tilted his head and looked to the ceiling.
She'd asked him when he would know he'd
made it. The moment had come. And all he
wanted to do was hold her hand and tell her.

*God, I'm trusting You. But if my prayers aren't enough, I'm getting some help.*

He dialed Marshall. "Hey, man, I'm at the hospital about an hour and a half away from Sweet Dreams. Kit's in trouble. I don't know what's wrong with her or how the baby is at this point, but there's a good chance I won't be able to make it to the wedding."

"I'm sorry, man. Don't worry about the wedding. Just stay there and take care of Kit. Hey, I had to miss Nash's wedding because Belle was having the quadruplets."

"Thanks, Marshall. I hate to do this to you. Will you ask everyone to pray for her and the little guy? I'm calling Clint and Nash now."

"Sure thing. We'll be praying for Kit and the baby. And for you."

He couldn't speak for a moment. His friends were too good to him.

"I hope today is everything you've dreamed of, Marsh."

"If it ends with Ainsley as my wife, it will be. Keep us posted." He hung up.

Wade called Nash and Clint and explained the situation. They promised to pray, too, and told him they'd check in now and then for updates.

He tossed the coffee cup in the trash and returned to his seat. What if Kit had taken a turn for the worse?

What if she lost the baby?

*God, let them both live. If You'll give me another chance, I'll never let her go. I'll tell her in no uncertain terms how much she means to me. I'll put a ring on her finger and break every speed limit to get to a church.*

*I need her, God.*

*I need her.*

# Chapter Fifteen

Gentle pressure on the inside of Kit's wrist made her eyelashes flutter. Muffled voices filled her groggy head, but only snippets made sense. Words like *pulse* and *temperature* and *blood pressure* were familiar. Other words? Not so much. She opened her eyes. Two concerned faces stared at her.

"You're awake." A nurse smiled.

She didn't know what to think. The events of the night were there, front and center, in her mind. But calm had overcome the earlier panic. She had the overwhelming feeling she'd be okay no matter what.

*God, my Father, I trust You.*

A strap covered her belly and cords led to a machine next to her. She couldn't see the display. A fetal monitor. The fact it was still hooked up filled her with hope.

*Lord, my baby is so precious to me. And I know he is to You, too. Whatever happens, give me a strength like Sandra's to hold on to my faith.*

"Please—" she reached for the nurse "— tell me if the baby made it."

A kick in her abdomen made her cover her mouth. He was alive! Tears streamed from her eyes. He kicked again, and she laughed and cried at the same time, rubbing her belly.

"I felt him," she said to the nurse. "He's in there. He's okay."

The nurse gave her a tender smile. "He's strong. We've been monitoring him since we brought you in. It was touch and go for both of you for a while, but we're glad to have you back."

"What happened?" She hugged both arms around her stomach as best as she could.

"You arrived unconscious with a high

fever. We tried to get your temperature down, but your body wasn't cooperating." The nurse motioned for a worker to get Kit something to drink.

"Do they know what's wrong? And did it hurt the baby?"

"I'll get the doctor. She'll explain everything." The nurse finished checking her vital signs and left the room.

Kit relaxed into the pillow. *Thank You, God! Thank You for saving my baby. And me. Your grace astounds me.*

"Hi, Kit, I'm Dr. Patel." The doctor's dark brown eyes and light brown skin contrasted with her black hair. Her smile lit her pretty face. "You have pyelonephritis—a severe kidney infection—and I'm happy to report you and your baby have passed through the most critical phase."

"So he'll be okay? Did you know he has a hole in his heart?" She massaged her tummy.

"No, I didn't know that. I don't think the infection would affect it. We'll send you down for an ultrasound later, but from the monitor, he seems to be doing fine."

Once more, relief poured through her. *Thank You, God. Thank You.*

"We're keeping you here for a few days. Expect lots of fluids, antibiotics and medicine to combat the fever." The doctor asked her a few questions and answered hers. "Are you hungry? The staff can bring you breakfast. I'll be back to check on you later."

A man in scrubs set two cups in front of her. "I brought you an ice water and a lemon-lime soda. Are you hungry?"

"No, but I need to see someone. My friend Wade Croft... If he's still here, will you bring him in?"

"I'll check. Be right back."

As soon as he left, she took a drink of the lemon-lime soda. Sweet cold perfection. It refreshed her parched throat. Her hand shook as she set it back on the tray.

Was Wade still here? She assumed he'd brought her to the hospital last night, but she didn't remember anything after calling him. How else could she have gotten here? Of course Wade had driven.

But wait…today was Marshall's wedding. The clock on the wall said it was almost eleven.

Where was she, anyhow? Sweet Dreams didn't have a hospital. What town was she in?

It didn't matter, because every hospital was over an hour from Sweet Dreams. Which meant by now Wade would be back at the ranch getting into his tux for the wedding.

She couldn't wait to thank him.

He'd saved her and the baby.

She wanted to do more than thank him. She had to tell him more. Needed to tell him more.

He might not love her the way she loved him, but she couldn't let another day go by without him knowing how important he was to her.

Wade had been her safety net for as long as she could remember. He hadn't asked for the job. Maybe he didn't even want it. But if it wasn't for Wade, she'd be adrift.

She could not do life without him.

She took another drink of the soda as jumbled Bible verses came to mind. God promised to never leave her or forsake her. God loved her. She knew it as surely as she knew she didn't deserve it.

A sense of calm whisked away the nervous energy.

*God, You've always been with me. I'll never be alone.*

When Wade came back—tonight, tomorrow, whenever—and if she got the courage to spell out everything—her feelings, her admiration, her love—would she be able to get through to him? Or had the trauma of his childhood killed any prospect of a real love and life together?

"She's asking for you." The receptionist tapped Wade's shoulder. Exhausted, he glanced up, registering that Kit must be okay if she was asking to see him.

*She's alive! Thank You, God. Thank You.*

"The baby?" he asked.

"I'm not at liberty to say." She turned and went back to the desk.

If Kit had lost the baby...

He couldn't bear the thought. The child he'd felt kicking had to live. He just had to.

Stiffly, he stood and went to find the room number the receptionist had given him. He had so much to say and no idea how to say it.

How could he adequately tell her everything in his heart?

He strode down the hall, ignoring the beeps and antiseptic smells. He'd gotten this far. He'd be here for her. He would hold her hand if the baby hadn't made it. He'd take care of her.

No matter what, he'd do whatever it took to make Kit understand the depth of his feelings.

Pausing in front of her door, he hauled his shoulders back, sent up a quick prayer for the right words and knocked.

Kit's eyes opened and grew wide. "You're here." She sounded breathless.

He covered the distance between them and sat in the chair next to her bed. Taking her hand in his, he caressed it, kissing the back of it.

"Of course I'm here. Where else would I be?" He kept his voice low. Flushed cheeks stood out in her pale face. "Tell me, Kitty Cat, did the baby… Is he okay?"

Her smile lit her eyes as she nodded. "He's fine. I'm having an ultrasound this afternoon, but the doctor thinks he'll be okay. He's been kicking ever since I woke up."

Emotion welled and Wade had to clench his teeth together and avert his eyes. The baby was okay. *You are a good God. Thank You.*

"Why aren't you at the wedding?"

The wedding? Did this woman have any idea how terrified he'd been of losing her?

"I would never leave your side, Kit." He stared into her eyes. "I was so scared. Scared of losing you. Scared of losing the baby."

Hope made her eyes shine greener than ever.

He pressed his lips to the back of her hand again.

"I was, too," she said. "When I felt him kick… It was the best feeling in the world."

"I can imagine." He attempted a smile. "Knowing you two are okay—well, that's the best feeling in the world for me. I've done a lot of thinking over the past twenty-four hours. And I realized a few things."

Her forehead wrinkled, but she didn't speak.

"I've been a big scaredy-cat, running away from the most important thing in my life. You." He waited for the choked-up feeling to subside. "It was easier for me to add to my ranch than it was for me to acknowledge reality. I've loved you since the day I met you. It started out innocent, and, as we grew older, I fought it tooth and nail every step of the way. I didn't want to open myself up to that kind of hurt. You and I both know what it's like to lose our loved ones. But the fact is I love you. Not as a foster brother. Not as a friend. I love you the way a man loves a woman. You mean more to me than a thousand ranches ever could. You could never be my roommate. You're my soul mate, Kit."

She stared at him, her mouth gaping open.

He continued. "I know this is a shock. I'm not trying to freak you out or anything, but I also can't wait another minute without telling you how I feel. I love your compassion, your sassy comebacks, your freckles, your smile. I love that you've always known what's most important—God and family— and you've never made any bones about wanting both. I love sitting on the porch with you, rocking and talking, or just sitting and watching the beauty of the land. I love your baby. Yes, your baby. I love your child like he's my own."

A river of tears ran down her cheeks, and he reached over and brushed them away with his thumb.

"Don't cry, Kit. I never want to make you cry."

"I'm not crying because I'm sad." She

wiped her eyes. "I just never expected to hear those words from you."

He blew out a breath. "Until yesterday, I didn't expect to admit them. You make me human, Kit. Without you, I'd be lost, thinking a ranch would fulfill me."

"You've always been human, Wade. You're the most giving person I know. I've been able to rely on you. No one else has ever offered me true security. But you? You've never let me down."

"You've always been my anchor."

"We can be each other's anchor—how does that sound?"

He squeezed her hand. "It sounds meant to be."

He had more to say. Including the things that made him squirm.

"Yesterday, when I proposed, I was a fool." He ducked his head. "I thought I could have it both ways—you and the baby without admitting my feelings for you. I didn't even want to admit them to myself. And I'm sorry, Kit. It was an insult. I hope you can forgive me."

"Hey," she said. He glanced up. "It wasn't an insult. It was the kindest gesture—"

"No, it wasn't. It was cowardly."

"It was generous. I'm used to feeling unwanted."

"I hope you never feel that way again. To me, you're the most important woman alive." He shifted his jaw. "I'm sorry. My offer was shabby. I don't blame you for turning me down."

"Oh, I didn't mean it like that… I'm botching this." She shook her head and rested it against the pillows. "Wade?"

"Yes?"

"Did you mean it? About loving me? And the baby?"

"More than anything."

"Why don't you ask me to marry you again?"

Kit held her breath as she watched the emotions playing across his face. He'd stayed! And he loved her! When he'd said he loved the baby like he was his own, she'd almost dissolved into a sobbing mess.

All the wonderful things he'd said…and he meant them. He did.

Wade rose from the chair, his blue eyes gleaming, then got down on one knee and took her hand in his.

"Kit McAllistor. My best friend. The girl who took me under her wing and never let me go. You are the love of my life. I don't want to spend a single minute without you. I want to take care of you. I want a ranch full of your babies. Please have mercy on this cowboy. Say you'll marry me."

A fleck of fear in his eyes made her heart skip a beat. She could barely grasp the wonders of the past hour. She was alive. The baby was alive. And Wade truly loved her and wanted to marry her—for real.

"Wade Croft. My best friend. The boy who protected me and never made me feel inferior. The man I cherish. You are the love of my life. You're the one who cared enough to cook for me, to drive me hours away to check out my living arrangements and not let me live in the worst apartment on earth. You offered me everything, and I want to give you the world in return. Yes, I will marry you. I want to have a ranch full of your babies, starting with this little one."

She placed her hand on her stomach, and he covered it with his. Then he leaned over, gently took her into his arms and whispered in her ear, "I love you. It's my mission to make you happy."

"Do you know what would make me happy?"

"What?"

"Kiss me and you'll get an idea."

His eyes darkened as a grin spread across his face.

"Gladly." He bent and claimed her lips with his.

This was what she'd been waiting for her entire life. She sank into his embrace, her pulse quickening as his mouth moved against hers. She tasted his need, his fears and a future full of love. In return, she poured her own need, hopes and desires into the kiss.

"Do you think it was always meant to be?" She traced his cheek with her finger.

"God works in mysterious ways." He kissed her lips once more. "Now tell me what happened to make you so sick. No one would fill me in on what was happening."

The poor man. She thought he already knew... "Well, apparently I have a severe kidney infection. Don't ask me to tell you the clinical name. I can't pronounce it. Anyway, it caused the fever and nausea and whatnot. They couldn't get the fever down until now."

"That was too close. I could have lost you." He sat back in the chair, scooting it as near as possible to the bed.

"All I could think of was the baby."

He held her hand and she got lost in his eyes.

"My friend—you know, the one who sent the baby items?—she wrote me a letter about losing three of her babies and having to trust God with their care. Believe it or not, it comforted me. Not right away. But as I woke sporadically, I felt this peace that no matter what happened, I would be okay, God would take care of us."

"I admire your faith. I never gave God credit for all my blessings. I guess it took almost losing you to make me realize how much I need Him."

"I do, too. I need Him every day."

"Kit?"

"Yes?"

"I made it."

"What?" What was he talking about? She tried to figure out what he meant, but couldn't.

"You asked me a while back when I'd know if I made it. I did. I have enough. I have more than enough. It's time to focus on what's really important."

A rush of emotion hit her.

"You're what's really important." His voice was low and it sent a shiver down her spine.

"You mean it, don't you?"

"Yes. I don't want a single day going by

without you being crystal clear how I feel about you. I love you. I thank God for you."

"I guess it's official."

"What?" His eyebrows formed a V.

"We both got our wishes from all those years ago. Except I'll never have the perfect family. It doesn't exist. I want to spend my life perfectly imperfect with you."

"Let's set the wedding date."

She laughed. "Speaking of weddings… shouldn't you head to Marshall's? I'm going to be stuck in the hospital for a few days. Why don't you go celebrate with him?"

"I'm not leaving your side."

She gave him a fake glare. "I'll probably be sleeping, anyhow."

"I'll consider going to the reception." He sighed. "After the ultrasound. I want to be there to hold your hand."

"Oh, Wade, that's why I love you."

"I'll be by your side for it all. The good. The bad. You can count on me. You can lean on me."

"I always have."

# *Epilogue*

"They should have been here by now." Kit angled her neck to look down the front hallway.

"They'll get here. Don't worry. The snow isn't too bad." Wade looked around his house, now truly a home. "They'll make kickoff."

Wade and Kit had invited their friends to JPX Ranch for some Sunday football. Clint, Lexi and their baby, Clara, had already arrived, and the rest of the crew would be here any minute. The aroma of taco meat hung in the air, making Wade's stomach growl.

"Oh, where is my head? I forgot to change

Jackson into his football outfit." Kit wiggled her fingers, indicating he should hand the baby over.

Wade cradled little Jackson to his chest and gave Kit puppy eyes. "But he's all snuggled in."

"I'll give him right back." Her eyes teased.

She was radiant. His. He still couldn't believe how quickly his life had changed since he'd proposed. It had taken them only a month to pull off a small wedding attended by their closest friends. The reception had been intimate, elegant and at Lexi's reception hall, the Department Store, like all their friends' weddings. A few months later his and Kit's pride and joy, Jackson, had arrived, at seven pounds and five ounces.

Every day felt like a new beginning with Kit as his wife. Jackson was developing like any other four-month-old baby. The sweet tyke had Wade wrapped around his finger and didn't even know it.

"Do you mind if I join you? Clara is

getting fussy." Lexi held the wiggly two-month-old.

"Of course not. Wade ordered matching gliders for the baby's room. We can chat in there."

Wade and Clint watched the women walk down the hall to the nursery he'd set up in one of the spare bedrooms.

"Any word from Nash?" Clint checked his watch. "The game's starting soon."

"They're probably exhausted. Colten's only a month old, and if he's anything like Jackson was when we brought him home, he's up all night."

Clint rubbed his eyes and yawned. "Yeah, Clara gets up every three hours. I know you'll probably rib me for this, but I like getting up with her. She's so tiny and cute."

"I'm not ribbing you, man. I hold Jackson every chance I get." Wade grinned.

"Did you hear back from the doctor about the hole in his heart?"

"Yeah, and it's good news, considering. They're running more tests and will be checking it when he turns six months, but the doctor thinks there's a strong chance the hole will close up on its own. If not, he'll have to have surgery. We've been assured this type of operation is routine."

"That's great, and in the meantime, we'll keep praying for his heart to heal."

A knock on the door got Wade to his feet. He hurried to the front entrance. Nash, Amy and Ruby, with Colten all bundled up in his carrier, were on the porch.

"It's about time you got here."

"Uncle Wade!" Ruby held her arms up, and he tossed her in the air.

"You're lighter than a feather, Ruby. Did you come to cheer on the team?"

She pulled a face. "I brought coloring books. I don't like football."

Voices and footsteps sounded on the porch.

"What's this about you not liking football?" Marshall asked, appearing in the doorway.

"Uncle Marshall!"

"You made it." Wade slapped him on the back and ushered him and Ainsley inside.

"I guess the gang's all here."

"The way it should be."

Colten let out a tiny cry. Amy lifted him out of his carrier.

"Ladies, Kit and Lexi are in the nursery. Feel free to join them."

Ainsley and Amy hugged, then took Colten down the hall, with Ruby leading the way.

The men all headed to the living room. Snow was falling outside and the football game would begin in ten minutes.

"This reminds me of the day we met." Wade tapped his chin. "Except for the snow."

"All we need are bunk beds." Nash grinned.

"And a hole in my sneaker." Clint pointed to his shoe.

"And a chip on my shoulder." Marshall pretended to brush lint off his shoulder.

"And here we are. Best friends. Married. With families. Living the dream."

"I couldn't ask for more." Wade closed his eyes and counted his blessings. He'd been given a lifetime of them. He truly was a blessed man.

* * * * *

*If you enjoyed Wade's story,*
*pick up these other books in the*
*Wyoming Cowboys miniseries*
*by Jill Kemerer:*

The Rancher's Mistletoe Bride
Reunited with the Bull Rider
Wyoming Christmas Quadruplets

Dear Reader,

Thank you for reading Wade and Kit's story. I'm a bit weepy that the Wyoming Cowboys series is coming to an end. I enjoyed getting to know Clint, Nash, Marshall and Wade, the best friends and foster brothers who found love in each book. I like to think of all of them growing closer in their friendships and raising faith-filled families. Sweet Dreams will always be dear to my heart. I wonder what Dottie Lavert would have nicknamed me if I went to her diner. What would your nickname be?

One of the themes that came up again and again as I wrote these books was worthiness. Are we worthy of love? We all have difficult times when it's easy to fall into a pit of despair, insecurity, disillusionment or bitterness. Don't worry. God has declared you worthy, and this is a free gift. Isn't that the best news? Hold tight to your faith in Him.

Thanks again for choosing my book. Please sign up for my newsletter to stay informed of my upcoming releases. Go to jillkemerer.com/newsletter for the simple form. I love to hear from you! Feel free to email me at jill@jillkemerer.com or write me at P.O. Box 2802, Whitehouse, Ohio, 43571.

May God bless you!
*Jill Kemerer*